James Hadley Chase and The Murder Room

>>> This title is part of The Murder Room, our series dedicated to making available out-of-print or hard-to-find titles by classic crime writers.

Crime fiction has always held up a mirror to society. The Victorians were fascinated by sensational murder and the emerging science of detection; now we are obsessed with the forensic detail of violent death. And no other genre has so captivated and enthralled readers.

Vast troves of classic crime writing have for a long time been unavailable to all but the most dedicated frequenters of second-hand bookshops. The advent of digital publishing means that we are now able to bring you the backlists of a huge range of titles by classic and contemporary crime writers, some of which have been out of print for decades.

From the genteel amateur private eyes of the Golden Age and the femmes fatales of pulp fiction, to the morally ambiguous hard-boiled detectives of mid twentieth-century America and their descendants who walk our twenty-first century streets, The Murder Room has it all. **>>>**

The Murder Room
Where Criminal Minds Meet

themurderroom.com

James Hadley Chase (1906–1985)

Born René Brabazon Raymond in London, the son of a British colonel in the Indian Army, James Hadley Chase was educated at King's School in Rochester, Kent, and left home at the age of 18. He initially worked in book sales until, inspired by the rise of gangster culture during the Depression and by reading James M. Cain's *The Postman Always Rings Twice*, he wrote his first novel, *No Orchids for Miss Blandish*. Despite the American setting of many of his novels, Chase (like Peter Cheyney, another hugely successful British noir writer) never lived there, writing with the aid of maps and a slang dictionary. He had phenomenal success with the novel, which continued unabated throughout his entire career, spanning 45 years and nearly 90 novels. His work was published in dozens of languages and over thirty titles were adapted for film. He served in the RAF during World War II, where he also edited the RAF Journal. In 1956 he moved to France with his wife and son; they later moved to Switzerland, where Chase lived until his death in 1985.

By James Hadley Chase
(published in The Murder Room)

The Vulture is a Patient Bird

James Hadley Chase

An Orion book

Copyright © Hervey Raymond 1969

The right of James Hadley Chase to be identified as the author of this
work has been asserted in accordance with the Copyright, Designs and
Patents Act 1988.

This edition published by
The Orion Publishing Group Ltd
Orion House
5 Upper St Martin's Lane
London WC2H 9EA

An Hachette UK company
A CIP catalogue record for this book is available from the British Library

ISBN 978 1 4719 0368 7

www.orionbooks.co.uk

Chapter One

His built-in instinct for danger brought Fennel instantly awake. He raised his head from the pillow and listened. Black darkness surrounded him: the darkness of the blind. Listening, he could hear the gentle slap-slap of water against the side of the moored barge. He could hear Mimi's light breathing. There was also a slight rhythmetic creaking as the barge heaved in the swell of the river. He could also hear rain falling lightly on the upper deck. All these sounds were reassuring. So why then, he asked himself, had he come so abruptly awake?

For the past month he had lived under the constant threat of death, and his instincts had sharpened. Danger was near: he felt it. He imagined he could even smell it.

Silently, he reached down and groped under the bed until his fingers closed around the handle of a police baton. Attached to the end of the baton was a short length of bicycle chain. This chain turned the baton into a deadly, vicious weapon.

Gently, so as not to disturb the sleeping woman at his side, Fennel raised the sheet and blanket and slid out of bed.

He was always meticulously careful to place his clothes on a chair by the bed: no matter where he stayed. To find his clothes, to dress quickly in the dark was vitally important when living under the threat of death.

He slid into his trousers and into rubber soled shoes. The woman in the bed moaned softly and turned over. Holding the flail in his right hand, he moved silently to the door. He had learned the geography of the barge and the solid darkness didn't bother him. He found the well greased bolt and drew it back, then his fingers found the door handle and turned it. Gently, he eased open the door a few inches. He peered out into the rain and darkness. The slapping sound of water against the side of the barge, the increased sound of the rain blotted out all other sounds, but this didn't deceive Fennel. There was danger out there in the darkness. He could feel the short hairs on the nape of his neck bristling.

Cautiously, he opened the door wider so that he could see the full length of the deck faintly outlined by the street lights of the embankment. To his left, he could see the glow of light from

1

London's West-end. Again he listened; again he heard nothing to alarm him. But the danger was there . . . he was sure of it. He crouched, lay flat and slid out on to the cold, wet deck. Rain pattered down on his naked, powerful shoulders. He edged forward, then his lips came off his even white teeth in a snarl.

Some fifty metres from the moored barge, he could see a rowing boat drifting towards him. There were four powerfully built men crouching in the boat. He could see the outline of their heads and their shoulders against the glow of the distant lights. One of the men was using an oar to direct the boat towards the barge: his movements were careful and silent.

Fennel slid further on to the deck. His fingers tightened on the handle of the flail. He waited.

It would be wrong to describe Fennel as courageous as it would be wrong to describe a leopard as courageous. The leopard will run when it can, but when cornered, it becomes one of the most dangerous and vicious of all jungle beasts. Fennel was like the leopard. If he saw a way out, he ran, but if he were trapped, he turned into a nerveless animal determined only . . . no matter the means . . . on self preservation.

Fennel had known sooner or later they would find him. Well, they were here, drifting silently towards him. Their approach left him only with a vicious determination to protect himself. He was not frightened. He had been purged of fear once he knew for certain that Moroni had decreed that he should die.

He watched the boat as it drifted closer. They knew he was dangerous, and they were taking no risks. They wanted to get aboard, make a quick dash down into the bedroom and then the four of them would smother him while their knives carved him.

He waited, feeling the rain cold on his naked shoulders. The man with the oar dipped the blade and made a gentle stroke. The boat heaved over the wind-swept water at a faster rate.

Fennel was invisible in the shadows. He decided he had judged his position accurately. They would board the barge about four metres from where he was lying.

The rower shipped the oar and laid it gently as if it were made of spun sugar along the three seats of the boat. He now had enough way to bring the boat to the side of the barge.

The man sitting on the front seat stood up and leaned forward. He eased the boat against the side of the barge, then with an athletic spring, he came aboard. He turned and caught the hand of the second man who moved forward. As he was helping him on to the deck, Fennel made his move.

He rose up out of the darkness, slid across the slippery deck and slashed with the flail.

The chain caught the first man across his face. He gave a wild yell, staggered, then pitched into the river.

The second man, his reflexes swift, spun around, knife in hand to face Fennel, but the chain slashed him around the neck, tearing his skin and sending him reeling back. He clutched at nothing, then went into the water, flat on his back.

Fennel darted into the shadows. His grin was vicious and evil. He knew the other two men in the boat couldn't see him. The light was behind them.

There was a moment of confusion. Then frantically, the man who had used the oar, grabbed it and began to pull away from the barge. The other man was trying to get his companions out of the river into the boat.

Fennel lay watching. His heart was hammering, and his breathing came in jerky snorts through his wide nostrils.

The two men were dragged aboard. The rower had the second oar now in the rowlock and was pulling away from the barge. Fennel remained where he was. If they saw him, they might risk a shot. He waited, shivering in the cold, until the boat disappeared into the darkness, then he got to his feet.

He leaned over the side of the barge to wash the blood off the chain. He felt the icy rain sliding down inside his trousers. He thought they might come back later, and if they did, the odds would be stacked against him. They would no longer be taken by surprise.

He shook the rain out of his eyes. He must get out, and get out fast.

He went down the eight steps into the big living and bedroom and flicked on the light.

The woman in bed sat up.

'What is it, Lew?'

He paid no attention to her. He stripped off his sodden trousers and walked naked into the small bathroom God! He was cold! He turned on the hot shower tap, waited a moment, then stepped under the healing hot spray.

Mimi came into the bathroom. Her eyes were drugged with

3

sleep, her long black hair tousled, her big breasts escaping from her nightdress.

'Lew! What is it?'

Fennel ignored her. He stood, thick, massive and short, under the hot spray of water, letting the water soak the thick hairs on his chest, belly and loins.

'Lew!'

He waved her away, then turned off the shower and took up a towel.

But she wouldn't go away. She stood outside the bathroom, staring at him, her green, dark ringed eyes alight with fear.

'Get me a shirt . . . don't stand there like a goddam dummy!'

He threw aside the towel.

'What happened? I want to know. Lew! What's going on?'

He pushed past her and walked into the inner room. He jerked open the closet door, found a shirt and struggled into it, found a pair of trousers and slid into them. He pulled on a black turtle neck sweater, then shrugged himself into a black jacket with leather patches on the elbows. His movements were swift and final.

She stood in the doorway, watching.

'Why don't you say something? Her voice was shrill. 'What's happening?'

He paused for a brief moment to look at her and he grimaced. Well, she had been convenient, he told himself, but no man in his right mind could call her an oil painting. Still, she had provided him with a hideout on this crummy barge for the past four weeks. Right now, without her plaster of make-up, she looked like hell. She was too fat. Those sagging breasts sickened him. Her anxious terror aged her. What was she . . . forty? But she had been convenient. It had taken Moroni four weeks to find him, but now it was time to leave. In three hours, Fennel thought, probably less, she would not even be a memory to him.

'A little trouble,' he said. 'Nothing. Don't get excited. Go back to bed.'

She moved into the room. The barge lifted slightly as the wind moved the river.

'Why are you dressing? What were you . . .'

'Just shut up, will you? I'm leaving.'

Her face sagged.

'Leaving? Why? Where are you going?'

He took a cigarette from the box on the table. He was feeling fine now after the hot shower and more assured, but he knew she was going to be a nuisance. She was horribly possessive. She needed his brutal love-making ... the reason why she had kept him there. She wasn't going to be shaken off easily.

'Get into bed,' he said. 'You'll catch cold.' Thinking: as if I give a damn. 'I have a phone call to make.'

She knew he was lying and she grabbed hold of his arm.

'You can't leave me! I've done everything for you. You're not to go!'

'For God's sake, shut up!' Fennel snarled and shoving her aside, he crossed the room to the telephone. As he dialled the number, he looked at his wrist-watch. The time was 03.50 hrs. He waited, listening to the steady burr-burr-burr of the ringing tone. There was a click and a sleepy voice demanded, 'W'o the 'ell is this?'

'Jacey? This is Lew.'

'Gawd! I was asleep!'

'This earns you twenty nicker,' Fennel said, speaking slowly and distinctly. 'Get your car. Meet me at the Crown pub, King's Road in twenty minutes, and I mean twenty minutes.'

'You crackers? Look at the time! W'ot's up? I'm not coming out. It's raining fit to drown a duck.'

'Twenty nickers ... twenty minutes,' Fennel said quietly.

There was a long pause. He could hear Jacey breathing heavily and imagined he could hear his greedy brain creaking.

'The Crown?'

'Yes.'

'The things I do! Well, okay. I'm on my way.'

Fennel replaced the receiver.

'You're not leaving!' Mimi's face blotched with red and her eyes were glaring. 'I won't let you leave!'

He ignored her and went swiftly to the dressing-table, jerked open a drawer and snatched up the essential articles he always kept there: a safety razor, a tube of brushless cream, a toothbrush, three packs of Players cigarettes and a haircomb. These he stowed away in his jacket pocket.

She again grabbed hold of his arm.

'I've done everything for you!' she wailed. 'You blasted jail-bird! Without me, you would have starved!'

He shoved her away and crossed the room to the mantelpiece

that framed a phony fireplace in which stood an electric stove. He took down a big Chinese teapot. The moment he touched it, she sprang forward and tried to take the teapot from him. Her eyes were wild, her long black hair hung over her face making her look like a demented witch.

'Take your hands off that!' she screamed.

The flickering evil in his washed out grey eyes should have warned her, but she was too frantic to stop him taking her savings to be warned.

'Take it easy, Mimi,' he said. 'I have to have it. I'll let you have it back ... promise.'

'No!'

She hooked her fingers and slashed at his face as her left hand wrenched at the teapot. Fennel jerked his head back, released the teapot and then savagely struck her on the side of the jaw. The force of the blow flung her backwards. She fell, her eyes rolling up and her head thudding on the floor. The teapot smashed to pieces as her grip was released and money spewed from it.

Fennel poked aside the pile of silver and picked up the small roll of ten pound notes. He didn't look at the unconscious woman. He put the money in his hip pocket, picked up his flail and went up on deck. As far as he was concerned his thirty days with Mimi were chalk marks on the blackboard now erased.

Rain was falling heavily, and the wind felt bleak against his face. He stood for some seconds looking at the embankment, letting his eyes become accustomed to the darkness. Nothing moved. He would have to take a chance, he thought, and ran the landing plank, from the barge, down to the wet tarmac. He slid down the plank, gained the dark shadows and again paused to listen. Again he heard nothing to alarm him. His fingers tightened on the flail and keeping close to the embankment wall, he walked silently to the distant steps that led to the upper embankment.

If Jacey was late, he could be sunk, he thought. They would have to stop the bleeding: the one who had been hit on the neck would bleed like a stuck pig. Then they would telephone Moroni and report failure. Moroni would get four or five men down there fast. Fennel decided he had a possible half-hour of freedom: certainly not more.

But he had no need to worry. As he reached the darkened

Crown public house, he saw Jacey's battered Morris pull up. He sprinted across the road, opened the car door and slid in.

'Back to your place, Jacey.'

'Wait a mo',' Jacey said. The street light lit up his aged, rat face. 'W'ot's on the move?'

Fennel gripped Jacey's thin wrist.

'Back to your place!' he snarled.

Jacey caught a glimpse of the vicious twist of the mouth and the half mad expression of contained rage. He grunted, engaged gear and set the Morris in motion.

Ten minutes later, the two men were in a small, shabbily furnished room, lit by a dusty, shadeless lamp that hung precariously from the dirty ceiling.

Jacey put a bottle of Black & White on the table and two glasses. He poured two stiff drinks and cradled his glass in his dirty hands while he regarded Fennel uneasily.

Jacey was a bookie's clerk and did any odd job for the lesser tearaways to earn extra money. He knew Fennel to be a major tearaway. He had met him in Parkhurst jail when they were serving sentences: Fennel for robbery with violence: Jacey for trying to pass badly forged ten shilling notes. When they had been released, they had kept in touch and Jacey had been flattered to have a big man like Fennel interested in him. But now he was sorry he had had anything to do with Fennel. He had heard through the underworld grapevine that Fennel had talked and five of Moroni's men had walked into a police trap. He knew Moroni had put the death sign on Fennel, but he was too greedy to pass up the chance of earning twenty pounds.

Fennel took out Mimi's roll of ten pound notes. He pulled off two and tossed them on the table.

'Freeze on to those, Jacey,' he said. 'I'm staying here for a couple of days.'

Jacey's ferret-like eyes widened. He didn't touch the money on the table.

'Can't 'ave you 'ere for two days, Lew. Ain't safe. They'll carve me if they find out you've been 'ere.'

'I can carve you too,' Fennel said softly. 'And I'm here.'

Jacey scratched his unshaven chin. His eyes darted about the room while he considered the situation and the risks. Moroni was probably in bed, asleep, but Fennel was here. Fennel could be as dangerous as Moroni.

'Okay, then ... two days ... not an 'our more,' he said finally.

'In two days, I'll be out of the country,' Fennel said. 'I've got a job. Maybe, I won't be coming back.' He finished his whisky and then walked into the inner room and over to the battered couch that served Jacey as a bed. He kicked off his shoes and lay down.

'You sleep on the floor, and turn that goddamn light off.'

'Go a'ead,' Jacey said bitterly. 'Make yourself at 'ome.'

He reached up and turned off the light.

A week previously, Garry Edwards had seen in the *Daily Telegraph* the following advertisement:

Experienced helicopter pilot required for a three week unusual assignment. Exceptionally high remuneration. Send career details and photograph. Box S. 1012.

He had re-read the advertisement and had brooded over it. He liked the two words *unusual* and *exceptional*. He was looking for unusual work and badly needed exceptional money, so without telling Toni, he had written a letter to Box S.1012, setting out the details of his past career which was as full of lies as a colander is full of holes. He had enclosed a passport photograph and had mailed the letter.

A week had passed, and he now had given up all hope of any exceptional remuneration and any unusual job. On this cold, wet February morning, he sat in Toni's small, untidy sitting-room with a cup of Nescafé by his side while he searched the *Situations Vacant* columns in the *Daily Telegraph.*

Garry Edwards was a tall, powerfully-built man of twenty-nine years of age. He was handsome in a rugged way, with humorous brown eyes and dark-brown hair worn fashionably long to his collar. His mouth could laugh easily or tighten to a dangerous thinness. As he sat on Toni's broken down settee, dressed, in a white beach wrap, his long narrow feet bare, the wall clock showed the time was 08.45 hrs.

Having searched the *Situations Vacant* columns carefully, he dropped the newspaper to the floor in disgust. Well, he would have to do something pretty soon, he told himself. He had exactly one hundred and thirty pounds, five shillings and seven pence before he had to ask Toni to support him, and this, he told himself without much conviction, he would never do.

He had run into Toni White on the Calais–Dover channel boat. Happily, she had been in the bar when he had embarked with two tough-looking French detectives who remained with him until the vessel was about to sail. When they had gone, and after Garry had waved cheerfully to them as they stood on the rain-swept quay to see the vessel leave the harbour – a wave they had stonily ignored – he had gone down to the first class bar for his first drink in three years.

Toni had been sitting on a bar stool, her micro-mini skirt scarcely covering her crotch, sipping a Cinzano bitter on the rocks. He had ordered a double Vat 69 with a dash and then had saluted her. She seemed the kind of girl a man could salute if the man had a way with him, and Garry certainly had a way with him.

Toni was twenty-two years of age, blonde, elfin-like with big blue eyes with dark, heavy eyelashes a cow would envy. Also, she was very, very chic.

She regarded Garry thoughtfully and with penetration. She decided he was the most sexy-looking man she had ever seen, and she had a hot rush of blood through her body. She wanted to have him: to be laid by him as she had never been laid before in her short, sensual life.

She smiled.

Garry knew women. He knew all the signs, and realized that here was an invitation that needed little or no finesse.

He had in his wallet the sum of two hundred and ninety pounds: what remained of the sale of his aircraft before the French police had caught up with him. He was full of confidence and raring to go.

He finished his drink, then smiling, he said, 'I would love to know you better. We have over an hour before we land. May I get a cabin?'

She liked his direct approach. She wanted him. His suggestion made everything simple. She laughed, then nodded.

It was easy to get a cabin, draw the curtains and lock themselves in. The steward had to rap a dozen times to remind them they had reached Dover and if they didn't make haste, they would miss the boat train.

While sitting by his side in an otherwise empty first class compartment on their way to London, Toni had told him she was a successful model, had plenty of work, had a two room apartment in Chelsea and if he wanted a roof . . . 'well, honey-love, why not move in?'

Garry had been planning on a cheap room in some modest hotel off the Cromwell Road until he could take stock and find himself lucrative employment. He didn't hesitate.

He had been living now with Toni for some three weeks, spending his remaining capital but not finding any lucrative employment. Now, with no prospects, he was getting slightly anxious. Toni, however, thought it all a huge joke.

'Why worry, you big gorgeous animal?' she had demanded the previous evening, jumping on to his lap and nibbling his ear. 'I have all the money in the world! Let's make hectic love!'

Garry finished his half-cold coffee, grimaced and then went to the window to stare down at the slow-moving traffic and at the stream of men and women, sheltering under umbrellas, hurrying to work.

He heard a sound at the front door: letters being dropped into the box.

Toni received many letters each morning from gibbering young men who adored her, but Garry hoped there just might be a letter for him. He collected fifteen letters from the box, flicked through them quickly and found one for himself. The deckled edge, handmade paper of the envelope was impressive. He ripped it open and extracted a sheet of paper.

The Royal Towers Hotel
London. W.1.
Would Mr. Garry Edwards please call at the above address on February 11th at 11.30 hrs. and ask for Mr. Armo Shalik. (Ref. Daily Telegraph. Box. S.1012).

Well, yes, Garry thought, he would certainly call on Mr Armo Shalik. With a name like that and with such an address there had to be a smell of money.

He took the letter into the small bedroom.

Toni was sleeping heavily. She lay on her stomach, her shortie nightdress rucked up, her long, lovely legs spread wide.

Garry sat on the edge of the bed and admired her. She really was delightfully beautiful. He lifted his hand and smacked her sharply on her bare rump. She squirmed, closed her legs, blinked and looked over her shoulder at him. He smacked her again and she hurriedly spun around and sat up.

'That's assault!' she declared. 'Where are my pants?'

He found them for her at the end of the bed and offered them. She regarded him, smiling.

'Do I need them?'

'I shouldn't have thought so,' Garry said with a grin. 'I've had a letter. Could you turn your indecent mind to business for a moment?'

She looked questioningly at him.

'What's cooking?'

He told her about the advertisement in the *Daily Telegraph*, that he had answered it, and now he had a reply. He gave her the letter.

'The Royal Towers! The newest and the best! What a lovely name! Armo Shalik! I smell bags and bags of gold and diamonds.' She tossed the letter into the air and threw her arms around Garry's neck.

Around 11.00 hours. Garry detached himself from Toni's clutch, took a shower and then dressed in a blue blazer and dark-blue Daks. He surveyed himself in the mirror.

'A little dark under the eyes,' he said, straightening his tie. But that is to be expected. Still, I think I look healthy, handsome and handmade . . . what do you think, you beautiful doll?

Completely naked, Toni was sitting in the armchair, sipping coffee. She regarded him affectionately.

'You look absolutely gorgeous.'

Garry picked her out of the armchair and fondled her. Having kissed her, he dumped her back in the chair and left the apartment.

At exactly 11.30 hrs. he approached the hall porter of the *Royal Towers Hotel* and asked for Mr. Armo Shalik.

The hall porter surveyed him with that blank expression all hall porters wear when they neither approve nor disapprove. He called a number, spoke quietly, then replaced the receiver.

'Tenth floor, sir. Suite 27.'

Garry was whisked up by the express lift to the tenth floor. He was conducted by the lift-man to the door of Suite 27. He was obviously too important and too fragile to knock on the door. The lift-man did this service, bowed and retired.

The smell of money, as far as Garry was concerned, was now over-powering.

He entered a small distinguished room where a girl sat behind a desk on which stood three telephones, an I.B.M. golf ball typewriter, an intercom and a tape-recorder.

The girl puzzled Garry because although she had a nice figure, was dressed in a stylish black frock, was beautifully groomed, her hair immaculate, she was nothing to him but a sexless photograph of a woman long since dead. Her blank face, her immaculately plucked eyebrows, her pale lipstick merely emphasized her lack of charm: a robot that made him feel slightly uncomfortable.

'Mr. Edwards?'

Even her voice was metallic: a tape-recording badly reproduced.

'That's me,' Garry said, and because he never liked to be defeated by any woman, he gave her his charming smile.

It had no effect. The girl touched a button, paused, then said, 'Mr. Edwards is here, sir.'

A green light flashed up on the intercom. Obviously, Mr. Shalik didn't care to waste his breath. He preferred to press buttons than to talk.

The girl got up, walked gracefully to a far door, opened it and stood aside.

Impressed by all this, Garry again tried his smile which again bounced off her the way a golf ball bounces off a brick wall.

He moved past her into a large sunny room, luxuriously furnished with period pieces and impressive looking paintings that could have been by the great masters but probably weren't.

At a vast desk sat a small, fat man, smoking a cigar, his chubby hands resting on the desk blotter. Garry judged him to be around forty-six years of age. He was dark-complexioned with close cut black hair, beady black eyes and a mouth that he used for food but not for smiles. Garry decided he was either an Armenian or an Egyptian. He had the stillness and the probing stare of power. As Garry walked slowly to the desk, the beady black eyes examined him. They were X-ray eyes, and by the time Garry had reached the desk, he had an uncomfortable feeling this fat little man knew him rather better than he knew himself.

'Sit down, Mr. Edwards.' The accent was a little thick. A chubby hand waved to a chair.

Garry sat down. He now regretted laying Toni an hour ago. He felt a little depleted and he had an idea that this fat little man wouldn't have much time for depleted applicants for the job he was offering. Garry sat upright and tried to look intelligent.

Shalik sucked in rich smelling smoke and allowed it to drift from his mouth like the smoke from a small, but active volcano. He picked up a sheet of paper which Garry recognized as his letter of application and he studied it for several moments, then he tore it up and dropped it into a hidden wastepaper basket.

'You are a helicopter pilot, Mr. Edwards?' he asked, resting his hands on the blotter and regarding the ash of his cigar with more interest than he regarded Garry.

'That's correct. I saw your ad and I thought . . .'

The chubby hand lifted, cutting Garry off.

'This nonsense you have written about yourself . . . at least, it proves you have imagination.'

Garry stiffened.

'I don't get that. What do you mean?'

Shalik touched off his cigar ash into a gold bowl at his elbow.

'I found your lies amusing,' he said. 'I have had you investigated. You are Garry Edwards, aged twenty-nine, and you were born in Ohio, U.S.A. Your father ran a reasonably successful service station. When you were sufficiently educated, you worked with your father and you came to know about motor cars. You and your father didn't get along. Probably faults on both sides, but that is of no interest to me. You had the opportunity to learn to fly: you took it. You have talent with machines. You got a job as an air chauffeur to a Texas oilman who paid you well. You saved your money. The job didn't interest you. You met a wetback smuggler who persuaded you to smuggle Mexicans into the States. The pay was good, and when the operation was over, you decided to go into the smuggling business. You went to Tangiers, bought your own aircraft and flew consignments of various contrabands into France. You prospered as smugglers do for a time. However, you became greedy as smugglers do and you made a mistake. You were arrested. Your co-pilot managed to get your plane in the air while you were struggling with the police. He sold your plane and banked the money for you to have when you came out of the French prison after serving a three year sentence. You were deported from France and you are here.' Shalik stubbed out his cigar and looked at Garry. 'Would you say my information is correct?'

Garry laughed.

'Dead on the nail.' He got to his feet. 'Well, it was a try. I won't take up any more of your time.'

Shalik waved him back to his chair.

'Sit down. I think you are the man I am looking for. You can satisfy me that you have a pilot's licence and that you can handle a helicopter?'

'Of course,' Garry returned and lugged out a plastic folder which he had brought along and laid it on the desk. Then he sat down again.

Shalik examined the papers which the folder contained. He took his time, then he returned the folder.

'Satisfactory.' He took another cigar from his desk drawer, regarded it carefully, then cut the end with a gold cutter. 'Mr. Edwards, am I right in thinking you would be prepared to handle a job that is not entirely honest so long as the money is right?'

Garry smiled.

'I'd like that qualified. What do you mean ... not entirely honest?'

'Difficult, unethical work that does not involve the police in any way, but pays handsomely.'

'Can you make it clearer than that?'

'I am offering three thousand dollars a week for a three-week assignment. At the end of the assignment you will be nine thousand dollars better off. There are certain risks, but I can promise you the police won't come into it.'

Garry sat upright. Nine thousand dollars!

'What are the risks?'

'Opposition.' Shalik regarded his cigar with indifferent, beady eyes. 'But life is made up of opposition, isn't it, Mr. Edwards?'

'Just what do I have to do to earn this money?'

'That will be explained to you tonight. You will not be alone. The risks and responsibilities will be shared. What I want to know now is if you are willing to do three weeks work for nine thousand dollars.'

Garry didn't hesitate.

'Yes ... I am.'

Shalik nodded.

'Good. Then you will come here at 21.00 hrs. tonight when I will introduce you to the other members of the team and I will explain the operation.' The chubby hand made a slight signal of dismissal.

Garry got to his feet.

'Please don't talk about this assignment to anyone. Mr. Edwards,' Shalik went on. 'You must regard it as top secret.'

'Sure . . . I'll say nothing.'

Garry left the room.

The girl at the desk got up and opened the door for him. He didn't bother to smile at her. His mind was too preoccupied. Nine thousand dollars! Wow!

The girl watched him enter the lift and then she returned to her desk. She sat for some moments, listening. Then hearing nothing from the inner room, she softly opened a drawer in her desk and turned off a small tape-recorder whose spools were conveying tape through the recording head.

Precisely at 21.00 hrs. Garry was shown into Shalik's office by the dark-haired girl who he knew now by the name-plate on her desk to be Natalie Norman.

There were two men sitting uneasily in chairs, smoking and waiting. They both looked closely at Garry as he took a chair. In his turn, he looked closely at them.

The man on his left was short and heavily built. He reminded Garry a little of Rod Steiger, the Oscar-winning movie star. His close cut woolly hair was white, his washed out grey eyes shifty. His thin lips and square chin hinted at viciousness.

The other man was some ten years younger: around Garry's age. He was of middle height, thin, his hair bleached almost white by the sun and his skin burnt to a dark mahogany. He wore a straggly moustache and long sideboards. Garry liked the look of him immediately, but disliked the look of the other man.

As he settled himself in the chair, a door at the far end of the room opened and Shalik entered.

'So you have all arrived,' he said, coming to his desk. He sat down and went through the ritual of lighting a cigar while he looked at each man in turn with intent, probing eyes. 'Let me introduce you to each other.' He pointed his cigar at Garry. 'This is Mr. Garry Edwards. He is a helicopter pilot and a car expert. He has spent three years in a French prison on smuggling charges.' The other two men looked sharply at Garry who stared back at them. The cigar then pointed to the younger man. 'This is Mr. Kennedy Jones who has flown from Johannesburg to attend this meeting,' Shalik went on. 'Mr. Jones is a safari expert. There is nothing he can't tell you about wild animals, South Africa in general and the fitting out of an expedition into the African bush. I might add Mr. Jones has had the misfortune to spend a few years in a Pretoria jail.' Jones stared up at the ceiling, a grin hovering around his humorous mouth. There was a pause, then Shalik went on, 'Finally, this is Mr. Lew Fennel who is an expert safe breaker . . . I believe that is the term. He is regarded by the police and the underworld as the top man in his so-called profession. He too has served a number of years in prison.' Shalik paused and looked at the three men. 'So, gentlemen, you have something in common.'

None of them said anything: they waited.

Shalik opened a drawer in his desk and took out a folder.

'The introductions concluded, let us get down to business.' He opened the folder and took from it a large glossy photograph. This he handed to Fennel who stared with puzzled eyes at the medieval diamond ring shown in the photograph. He shrugged and passed the photograph to Garry who in turn passed it to Jones.

'You are looking at a ring,' Shalik said, 'designed by Caesar Borgia.' He looked at the three men. 'I take it you all know of Caesar Borgia?'

'He's the guy who poisoned people, wasn't he?' Fennel said.

'I think that is a fair description. Yes, among many other things, he poisoned or caused to be poisoned a number of people. This ring you see in the photograph was designed by Borgia and made by an unknown goldsmith in 1501. To look at the ring, it would be hard to believe that it is a lethal weapon, but that is what it is . . . a very lethal weapon. It works in this way. There is a tiny reservoir under the cluster of diamonds and this reservoir was filled with a deadly poison. In the cluster of diamonds is a microscopic hollow needle of exceptional sharpness. When Borgia wished to get rid of an enemy, he had only to turn the ring so the diamonds and needle were worn inside and he had only to clasp the hand of his enemy to inflict a small scratch. The enemy would be dead in a few hours.

'The ring was lost for four centuries. It turned up in the effects

16

of a Florentine banker who died with his wife and family in a car crash a couple of years ago. His effects were sold. Fortunately, an expert recognized the ring and bought it for a song. It was offered to me.' Shalik paused to tap ash off his cigar. 'Among my various activities, I buy *objets d'art* and sell them to wealthy collectors. I knew of a client who specialized in Borgia treasures. I sold him the ring. Six months later, the ring was stolen. It has taken me a long time to find out where it is. It was stolen by agents working for another collector who has acquired, through these agents, probably the finest collection of art treasures in the world. This operation, Gentlemen, which I am asking you to handle, is for you three to recover the ring.'

There was a long pause, then Fennel, sitting forward, said, 'You mean we steal it?'

Shalik looked at Fennel with distaste.

'Putting it crudely, you could say that,' he said. 'I have already pointed out there is no question of police inter‐ ference. This collector has stolen the ring from my client. You take it from him. He is in no position to complain to the police.'

Fennel let his cigarette ash drop on the rich Persian carpet as he asked, 'How valuable is this ring?'

'That doesn't concern you. It is, of course, valuable, but it has a specialized market.' Shalik paused, then went on, 'I will tell you a few details about the man who now has the ring. He is enor‐ mously rich. He has a compulsive urge to own the finest art treasures he can lay his hands on. He is utterly unscrupulous. He has a network of expert art thieves working for him. They have stolen many *objets d'art* from the world's greatest museums, and even from the Vatican, to fill his museum which is without doubt the finest in the world.'

Feeling he should make a contribution to this discussion, Garry asked, 'And where is this museum?'

'On the borders of Basutoland and Natal . . . somewhere in the Drakensberg mountains.'

Kennedy Jones leaned forward.

'Would you be talking about Max Kahlenberg?' he asked sharply.

Shalik paused to touch off his cigar ash.

'You know of him?'

'Who doesn't, who has lived in South Africa?'

17

'Then suppose you tell these two gentlemen what you know about him.'

'He's the man who has the ring?'

Shalik nodded.

Jones drew in a long, slow breath. He rubbed his jaw, frowning, then lit a cigarette. As he exhaled smoke, he said, 'I only know what is common knowledge. Kahlenberg is a bit of a mythical figure on which all kinds of weird rumours stick. I do know his father, a German refugee from the First World War, struck it rich, finding one of the biggest gold mines just outside Jo'burg. Old Karl Kahlenberg was shrewd and no fool. He invested well and milked his mine dry. From what I hear, he ended up with millions. He married a local girl when he was over sixty years old. He married because he wanted a son to carry on his name. He got his son: Max Kahlenberg. There was a real mystery about the birth. No one except the doctor and the nurse saw the baby. There was a rumour it was a freak ... some even said it was a monster. Anyway, no one ever set eyes on the baby. The old man died in a hunting accident. Mrs. Kahlenberg moved from Jo'burg and built a house in the heart of the Drakensberg range. She continued to keep her son hidden, cutting herself off from all social contacts. She died some twenty years ago. Max Kahlenberg remains a recluse. He is supposed to be as clever as his father. He has enlarged the house his mother built. He has around one hundred square miles of jungle surrounding the house and he employs a number of trained Zulus to keep hikers, tourists and gapers away from the house.' Jones paused, then leaning forward, stabbing his finger into the palm of his hand, he went on, 'From what I've heard, getting near Kahlenberg's place would be like trying to open an oyster with your fingers.'

Again there was a long pause, then Fennel crushed out his cigarette and looked at Shalik, his eyes narrowed.

'Is what he says right?'

Shalik lifted his fat shoulders.

'A fairly accurate statement,' he said. 'I have never said that this is an easy assignment. After all, I am paying very well. The approach to Khalenberg's house is not easy, but not impossible. I have a considerable amount of information which will help you.'

'That's fine,' Fennel said with a little sneer, 'but suppose we get to the house ... how do we get in?'

'Although Mr. Jones has a fair knowledge of Kahlenberg's

background,' Shalik said. 'He has omitted – or perhaps he doesn't know – the fact that although Kahlenberg is a cripple, he is fond of beautiful women.' He leaned back in his chair. 'Every fortress has its soft underbelly if you know where to look for it. I have a woman who will act as your Trojan Horse. If she can't get you into Kahlenberg's house, no one can.'

He pressed a button his desk.

There was a long pause, then the door behind Shalik opened and the most sensational, beautiful woman any of the three men, gaping at her, had ever seen, came slowly into the room and paused by Shalik's desk.

Chapter Two

Some ten years ago, Armo Shalik, sick of his small way of life, let it be known by a discreet advertisement in an Egyptian newspaper that he was prepared to undertake for a reasonable fee any assignment that presented difficulties. He received only one answer to his advertisement, but it was enough, since his client was an Arabian Prince who wished to have inside information concerning a future oil deal between a rival of his and an American oil company. By using the Prince's money and his own brains, Shalik obtained the information. The deal netted him $10,000, a modest enough fee, but the Prince was grateful, and he passed the word around that if you were in difficulties, if you wished for inside information, Shalik was the man to consult.

The following year with the capital he had saved, Shalik moved to London. He acquired a small list of extremely wealthy clients who continually consulted him. Money, of course, was no object. Shalik's fees rose sharply, but he always delivered. Among his clients were three Texas oil millionaires, four Arabian princes, two enormously wealthy American women, a Greek shipping tycoon and a number of British, French and German industrialists.

He was often to say, 'Nothing is impossible with unlimited money and brains.' He would pause to stare at his client. 'You will supply the money . . . I the brains.'

Armo Shalik prospered. In the early days, he considered whether to have a permanent staff to work under him, but he decided this was economically unsound. Shalik never wasted a dime. To keep a staff of experts on his payroll would mean half of them most of the time would be drawing on his money and doing nothing. He decided to fit men and women to the job when the job arrived. He discovered a not too scrupulous Detective Agency who were prepared not only to recommend likely applicants without asking awkward questions, but also to screen them, giving him intimate details of their background. It was in this way that he had found Lew Fennel, Kennedy Jones and Garry Edwards.

His permanent staff was small: consisting of Natalie Norman who acted as his receptionist and personal assistant, and George Sherborn who was his private secretary and valet.

But Shalik soon found that his assignments became more complicated and therefore more lucrative, he needed a woman in the field to be permanently at his disposal: a woman who had to be trained to work with and for him: a woman of exceptional talents and exceptional looks. Such a woman could be more useful to him than a dozen male experts. During the past years, he had hired a number of women to work with his experts, but more often than not they had failed him: either losing their nerve at a crucial moment or becoming sentimentally attached to the men they were working with, and this was something Shalik abominated.

So he set out to find a woman he could train to become his ideal woman operator. She had to be beautiful, perfectly built, talented and to be prepared to dedicate herself to his work.

Shalik travelled extensively, and while visiting the major cities of the world, he was constantly on the look-out for the woman he needed. He came across several likely applicants, but when he approached them, they either would have nothing to do with his proposition or proved to be beautiful but brainless. After some six months, he began to despair, wondering if he had set his sights too high.

Then one day he had a letter from one of his rich, spoilt

THE VULTURE IS A PATIENT BIRD

women clients, living in Tokyo, who asked him to buy her a leopard skin coat, a mink stole and a broadtail coat for evening wear. He was to get these furs from Finn Larson, a Copenhagen furrier who had her measurements and knew exactly what she required. Since the woman paid Shalik $21,000, a year as a retaining fee and since he charged fifteen per cent on all purchases made on her behalf and since he was in need of a brief vacation, he was happy to oblige.

Natalie Norman telephoned Finn Larson in Copenhagen to alert him that Shalik was coming and what he wanted. She was told that there was to be a lunch held at L'Angleterre Hotel for a number of Larson's special clients when models would display his furs and the clients would eat interesting Danish food. Larson hoped Mr. Shalik would attend.

Shalik arrived at the hotel the following day and went to the private room that Larson used for his excellent lunches and was welcomed by Larson, a balding, heavily-built Dane who gripped his hand and led him to a table before hurrying away to welcome yet another of his clients.

While Shalik was eating his lunch, girls came in to display Larson's beautiful furs.

Then suddenly, as a girl swept in, wearing a magnificent leopard skin coat, Shalik paused in his eating. After six months of searching, this was his moment of truth. He was certain this time this was the girl he was looking for.

Above average height, with tawny hair, hanging in silken waves to her shoulder blades, this girl – possibly twenty-six or so years of age – was the most sensationally, sensually beautiful feminine creation he had ever seen. Her jade green eyes, her full lips that gave promise of sexual excitement, her long tapering legs, her slim lovely hands made a picture of a male dream of desirability.

Shalik lost interest in his lunch as he watched her move with the arrogant walk of a trained model to the end of the room. She turned and walked back past him. He scarcely glanced at the leopard skin coat. When she had gone, to be replaced by another girl, wearing a seal skin coat, Shalik beckoned to Larson who came over.

'I'll take the leopard skin coat,' Shalik said. 'It is for Mrs. Van Ryan.' He paused, then looked up and asked, 'Who is the girl who modelled the coat?'

Larson smiled.

'Almost as magnificent as my coat, don't you think? She is Gaye Desmond ... An American freelance model who comes here from time to time. I use her for my leopard skins ... no other girl has such flair to show off leopard.'

Shalik took out his wallet, extracted his card and handed it to Larson.

'Would you be so kind as to give her my card?' he asked. 'I believe I can employ her should she need employment. You might mention to her who I am.' Shalik regarded Larson. 'You know, Mr. Larson, I am always serious. This is strictly business. You will be doing the girl a favour.'

Larson, who knew Shalik, had no hesitation.

Later, while Shalik was sitting in his suite, reading a complicated legal document, the telephone bell rang.

He lifted the receiver.

'This is Gaye Desmond.' He liked her rich contralto voice. 'You sent me your card.'

'Thank you for ringing, Miss Desmond. I have a proposition I would like to discuss with you. Could we have dinner together at the Belle Terresse, Tivoli, at 21.00 hrs?'

She said yes, and hung up.

She arrived punctually which pleased Shalik, and together they went to a table on the terrace that overlooked the lighted pool and the flowers that make Tivoli famous.

'It is a pity we didn't meet in Paris, Miss Desmond,' Shalik said as he began to examine the menu. 'The food here is indifferent. In Paris I could have offered you a meal worthy of your beauty.'

She was wearing a simple blue dress with a mink stole. Diamonds glittered at her ears as she tossed her tawny coloured hair back from her shoulders.

'I believe in eating what a country offers,' she said. 'Why yearn for better food in Paris when you are in Copenhagen?'

Shalik liked that. He nodded.

'So what will you have?'

She had no hesitation, and this also pleased Shalik. Women who stare vacantly at a menu and can't make up their minds bored him.

She chose Danish shrimps and the breast of duck in wine sauce. Having taken a little longer to examine the menu, Shalik

22

decided her choice was not only safe, but sound. He ordered the same.

'Miss Desmond,' Shalik said when the waiter had gone. 'I am looking for a woman to help me in my work. I am a rather special agent who looks after extremely wealthy, spoilt people, clever business men and even princes. I boast that nothing is impossible. Nothing is impossible if you have money and brains.' He paused, regarding her. 'However, I believe my work would be made easier if I had a woman like yourself working for me permanently. I must warn you it would be exacting work: sometimes dangerous, but always within the law of the country in which I operate.' This statement was untrue. Recently, Shalik had pulled off a number of illegal currency deals in London that could have landed him in jail had they been discovered, but Shalik's philosophy was that so long as he wasn't found out, any deal was within the law. 'The pay will be good. You will have your own apartment at the Royal Towers Hotel in London, paid by me. You will have many opportunities to travel.' He regarded her with his black, beady eyes. 'And I assure you, Miss Desmond, this will be a strictly business association.'

The tiny, pink, delicious shrimps now arrived with slices of toast, and there was a pause.

While Gaye buttered her toast, she asked, 'What makes you imagine I am suitable for such a post, Mr. Shalik?'

Shalik nibbled at his shrimps. He regretfully avoided the toast. He was four kilos overweight and was determined to make a sacrifice.

'Instinct, I suppose. I think you are just the woman I am looking for.'

'You say the pay will be good . . . just what does that mean?'

He ate another three shrimps before saying, 'Suppose you tell me about yourself. I can then make a valuation.'

She sipped the chilled Hock and regarded him with her green eyes: thoughtful, shrewd, calculating eyes that pleased him.

'Well . . .' She suddenly smiled and her smile lit up her face, making it gay and charming. 'As you can see, I am beautiful. I am intelligent. You will discover this. I speak French, Italian and Spanish fluently. I can get along in German. I was practically born on a horse. My father bred horses in Kentucky. I ski well. I can handle a sailing boat and, of course, any kind of motorboat. I have been a racing driver and there is nothing I don't know about cars. I understand men and what they what. Sex doesn't frighten me. I know how to please men if ... and only if ... I have to. I earn a comfortable living modelling specialized clothes, but I like money and want to make more.'

Shalik finished his shrimps and then stroked his thick nose.

'Is that all?'

She laughed.

'Isn't it enough?'

'Yes, I think so. Can you handle firearms?'

She lifted her eyebrows.

'Why should I need to?'

'Since you are otherwise so well equipped, I think you should have weapon training and also training in self-defence. This I can arrange. When a woman is as beautiful as you and when she may have to mix with dubious types of men, it is sound for her to understand the art of self-defence.'

They paused while the waiter served the duck and poured a Margaux '59 which Shalik had ordered in a moment of recklessness. The price was outrageous, but the wine excellent.

'Now it is your turn,' she said. She cut into the duck and grimaced. 'It's tough.'

'Of course. What did you expect? This is Copenhagen, not Paris.' He looked at her across the candle-lit table. 'My turn ... for what?'

'Your turn to make a valuation. I've told you about myself. Value me.'

Shalik liked her direct approach.

'If you are prepared to do exactly what I tell you, Miss Desmond,' he said as he began to cut the duck into small pieces. 'If you are prepared to be at my beck and call for eleven months in each year ... the remaining month will be yours to do as you wish. If you are prepared to take a course in self-defence, then I will pay you $10,000 a year with a one per cent cut on whatever I make on assignments you help me with. At a rough guess this should net you $25,000 a year.'

She drank a little of the Margaux.

'At least the wine is good, isn't it?'

'It should be, at the price they charge for it,' Shalik said sourly. He hated wasting his money. 'What do you say?'

She toyed with her glass as she considered his proposal, then she shook her head.

'No ... I am not interested. I could become an old man's mistress for twice that sum. You are asking me to hand myself over to you as a slave for eleven months, leading no life of my own during those months, to be entirely at your beck and call.' She laughed. 'No, Mr. Shalik, that is no kind of a price for what you are offering.'

Shalik would have been disappointed if she had said otherwise.

'So ... suppose you tell me under what conditions you will work for me?'

He was pleased she told him without hesitation.

'$30,000 a year whether I work or not, and five per cent of whatever you make in the deals in which I am concerned.'

Shalik shook his head slowly and sadly.

'Then I'm sorry, Miss Desmond. I must look elsewhere.'

They looked at each other and she gave him a charming smile, but he saw there was a jeering light in her eyes.

'Then I'm sorry too. So I must also look elsewhere.'

Shalik now knew she was the woman he was looking for and he settled down to bargain, but here he found his master and this pleased him. He hated to be defeated, but he realized if she could defeat him, the men she would have to mix with at his bidding would be as pawns in her hands.

At the end of the meal, and after Shalik had paid the outrageous bill, they had come to an agreement. A basic salary of $30,000 a year, plus four per cent of Shalik's earnings which involved her co-operation, to be paid into a Swiss bank, tax free, which Shalik decided ruefully would net her at least seven per cent of his take.

Once this was agreed, she came to London and went through a self-defence course that Shalik arranged for her. Her instructors were delighted with her.

'This woman is now highly proficient in defending herself,' they told Shalik. 'She can cope with any emergency.'

Completely satisfied with his find, Shalik installed her in a small suite on the floor below his at the Royal Towers Hotel, and within two months she had quickly proved her worth.

She handled two assignments not only successfully, but with a polish that delighted Shalik. The first assignment was to obtain a chemical formula required by a rival company. The second assignment was to obtain advance information about a big shipping merger which netted the client a considerable profit on the Stock

Market: part of which he handed to Shalik. In both cases, Gaye had had to sleep with the two men who supplied the information required. Shalik asked for no details. He was only too pleased to turn the information she gave him into cash.

Now, she had worked for him for six months and she had more than earned her basic salary.

Delighted with her, he had sent her off on a skiing vacation. He was sure she hadn't gone alone, but what was left of her private life was no concern of his. Then the Borgia ring affair came up and he had sent a telegram to Gstaad telling her to return immediately.

She returned by the first available aircraft and when she walked into his office, burned golden brown by the Swiss sun, her tawny hair around her shoulders, Shalik thought she looked magnificent.

He explained about the Borgia ring and was pleased by her interest.

'You will like Natal,' he said. 'The country is splendid. The three men who will work with you are all experts and should present no difficulties for you.' He stared at his evenly burning cigar. 'I think I should warn you that there are risks. Kahlenberg is dangerous.'

She shrugged her beautiful shoulders. Her smile was confident.

'Many men are dangerous,' she said quietly, 'so are many women.'

As Gaye Desmond paused beside Shalik, the three men got to their feet. While Shalik introduced them, Gaye regarded them searchingly. She liked the look of Kennedy Jones. She decided he was harmless and would be easy to handle and could be fun. Her green eyes swept over Fennel. This man was not only dangerous but he could be tricky to handle. Her experience of men and the expression in his washed out grey eyes as he looked at her, told her sooner or later, there would have to be a showdown with him. Then she took in Garry Edwards who was looking at her with an appreciative expression that she found flattering and pleasing. He was all right, she decided. Well, they were a mixed bunch to travel with, but at least two of them could be handled. The fat one was bound to be a nuisance.

'This is Miss Gaye Desmond . . . our Trojan Horse,' Shalik said.

'That I love,' Gaye laughed. 'I would rather be Helen than the horse.'

'Sit down, please.' Shalik drew up a chair for Gaye. 'Miss Desmond will travel with you. You will be flying to Johannesburg on Tuesday. I have arranged for your rooms at the Rand International hotel. You will stay there until Mr. Jones has organized the expedition. I have also arranged for the hire of a helicopter which Miss Desmond and Mr. Edwards will use.' He touched ash off his cigar, then went on, 'I have managed to obtain a certain amount of information about Kahlenberg's place, but none of this information is completely reliable. Before you can hope to get at the ring, it is essential for Miss Desmond to get into Kahlenberg's house and check the information I have obtained: this information is to do with various security measures and where the museum is located. Miss Desmond will pose as a professional photographer after wild game. I have arranged that she is credited to Animal World which is a sound, small American magazine for whom I have done past favours. It is possible that Kahlenberg might check, and it would be stupid not to be covered. Mr. Edwards will be her professional pilot. A helicopter is the ideal machine from which to get photographs of wild animals. Kahlenberg has an airfield. You two . . .' Here Shalik looked at Gaye and Garry, 'will land on the airfield. Your story will be that you saw the house from the air and can you take photographs? You will be refused, of course, but I am certain Kahlenberg will want to meet Miss Desmond.'

'But suppose he doesn't?' Garry said.

Shalik frowned at him.

'I said I was certain, and that means he will. I don't use words lightly.' The snub administered, Shalik went on, 'I have no idea where the museum is. I imagine it must be somewhere in the house which is a vast one storey building. As the museum contains many stolen treasures, it will be well hidden and well guarded. One of my agents in Durban, some eight years ago, happened to be watching a ship unload and noticed a considerable number of crates coming ashore with Kahlenberg's name on them. Knowing I was interested in Khalenberg, he investigated. The crates came from Bahlstrom of Sweden who you may know are the best safe makers and security experts in the world.' He glanced at Fennel. 'Am I telling you anything new?'

Fennel grinned.

'I know all about Bahlstrom. Years ago, I worked for them. They are good.'

'Yes, Mr. Fennel,' Shalik said. 'This is the main reason why I am hiring you.' He again touched off his cigar ash and continued, 'Fortunately, my agent was intelligent. He obtained a copy of the invoices from the shipping agent at some cost and sent it to me. I give it to you now to examine. It is possible with your knowledge of Bahlstrom's security system and with these invoices, you may get some idea of Kahlenberg's security set-up.' He handed a plastic envelope to Fennel who glanced at it and then shoved it in his hip pocket. 'You have until Monday morning to let me know what you think.'

'Okay,' Fennel said, crossing one fat leg over the other. 'I'll tell you.'

Shalik turned to Garry.

'Mr. Edwards, I have aerial maps of the Drakensberg range and of Kahlenberg's estate.' Again another plastic envelope passed across the desk. 'I will want you to tell me if you can land the helicopter from a place chosen by Mr. Jones on the Kahlenberg airfield. This we will also discuss on Monday.'

Garry nodded, taking the envelope.

Shalik now turned to Kennedy Jones.

'You will be responsible for fitting out the expedition and for transport. You and Mr. Fennel will go by road while Miss Desmond and Mr. Edwards fly. You can spend what you like but you must insure against the many difficulties which you could meet on the way in. The route to Kahlenberg's estate is exceptionally difficult at this season when the rains can be expected. But this is your affair. You will also have to find a way through the circle of Zulus who guard the approaches. You are the expert, so I don't propose making any suggestions.'

'I'll take care of it,' Jones said.

'Well then, we will have our final meeting on Monday,' Shalik said. 'We will then clear up the final details. Any questions?'

Fennel leaned forward.

'How about some money? We are being paid nine thousand each for this caper, but how about something in advance?'

Shalik made a grimace that could pass for as a smile.

'I was expecting that request from you.' He took from a drawer four envelopes and handing one to Gaye, he passed the other three across his desk. 'You will find in each envelope blank

Travellers Cheques to the total of $3,000. When you have successfully completed your mission, you will get the balance.' He glanced at his gold Omega. 'Then we meet here at 09.30 hrs. on Monday.'

Gaye left the room by the door behind Shalik. Garry and Ken Jones watched her going with regret. They started towards the far door as Fennel got to his feet.

'Mr. Fennel . . .'

Fennel looked at Shalik.

'There are a few additional things to discuss without wasting the time of these other gentlemen,' Shalik said quietly.

Fennel shrugged and sat down again. Shalik waved to the other two, dismissing them.

When they had gone, Shalik selected another cigar, clipped the end and lit it while he looked stonily at Fennel.

'It is necessary, Mr. Fennel, to have a straight talk with you. Your two companions have both served jail sentences, but you can hardly describe them as criminals. However, you are not only a criminal, but a dangerous and vicious one. I have selected you for this operation because of your expertise, but don't imagine I am ignorant of your criminal background. I know you are on the run and anxious to get out of England. You betrayed five criminals in order to reduce your own sentence and the leader of this gang – a man called Moroni – has sworn to kill you. An attempt was made last night, but failed. The second attempt might not fail.' Shalik paused to stare at Fennel who was now sitting up straight, his eyes glittering. 'So from what I am telling you, Mr. Fennel, you will see I keep myself well informed about the people I employ. Now I have received additional information about you. You are wanted for three vicious murders in Hong Kong, Cairo and Istanbul. Two of your victims were females: the third was a male prostitute. I have evidence of these crimes that Interpol would gladly receive. Does all this that I am telling you, Mr. Fennel, interest you?'

Fennel moistened his lips with his tongue.

'Are you threatening me? I got the idea we are working together.'

'Yes . . . we are working together, but that doesn't mean I can't threaten you. There are two things you are to keep constantly in mind.' Shalik pointed his cigar at Fennel. 'The first point is you will leave Gaye Desmond strictly alone. As soon as she came into this room, your disgusting mind began to wonder about her. You were thinking that in the African bush you would have opportunities to behave in the animal way that comes naturally to you. So I am warning you: try something like that with Miss Desmond, and I promise you Interpol will have your dossier from me. Is that clear?'

Fennel forced an uneasy grin.

'You hold the aces,' he said with an attempt at bravado. 'You are reading me wrong, but okay, so she is like my mother.'

Shalik grimaced.

'If you will excuse the personal remark . . . I feel sorry for your mother.'

Fennel gave a hard, barking laugh.

'You don't have to. She was one of the smartest thieves in the racket. If you want to be sorry for anyone, be sorry for my old man. He cut this throat when they put my mother away for ten years.'

'I am not interested in your family history,' Shalik said curtly. 'My second point is this. I want this ring. The operation won't be easy, but a man of your experience and ruthlessness should be able to handle it. However, if you fail, I see no reason why I shouldn't pass your dossier to Interpol . . . so you must understand that I will not tolerate failure.'

Fennel bared his teeth in a snarling grin.

'I'll get the goddam ring for you, but if so much depends on me, how about some extra money?'

'I will consider that when I have the ring. Now get out!'

Fennel stared at him, but Shalik was reaching for the telephone. As he began to dial a number, Fennel got up and went into the inner room where Natalie Norman was typing. He didn't look at her, but went out into the corridor and to the lift.

When he had gone, and when she was satisfied she could hear Shalik talking on the telephone, she turned off the hidden tape-recorder and removed the spool.

Garry shut himself in a telephone booth and called Toni who answered immediately.

'We're celebrating, chicken,' he said. 'I'm hungry. Meet me at the Rib Room, Carlton Towers in exactly one hour from this minute,' and he hung up cutting off her squeal of excitement.

He knew he had to give her at least an hour to get ready. Toni was a languid and slow dresser. By the time he reached the Rib Room he was pleasantly high, having drunk four vodka martinis in the bar of the Royal Towers Hotel.

Ken Jones had left him, saying he had a date with a girl friend. They had paused in the crowded lobby of the hotel and Jones had asked, 'What do you think of it all?'

'It's a job and the money's nice,' Garry returned. 'You and I will get along. I feel that. It's Fennel . . .'

Jones grinned.

'What are you worrying about? You have Gorgeous and a chopper. I have Fennel.'

'Well, watch him.'

'You bet . . . so long, see you Monday. Happy bed bouncing,' and Jones went off into the cold, wet night.

Toni, looking ravishing, turned up at the Rib Room just when Garry was losing patience.

'I'm damn well starving,' he complained. 'You're late!'

'I know, sweetie, but I just can't help it.' She flicked her long eyelashes at him. 'Like me?'

But now Garry had met Gaye Desmond, Toni White seemed suddenly a little young, trying a little too hard, and less exciting.

'You're wonderful.' The four martinis gave his voice conviction.

They moved into the restaurant. As they sat down, Toni asked, 'So you got the job?'

'You don't imagine we would be here if I hadn't?'

'Let's order and then you tell me, huh?'

'Don't say huh . . . only American businessmen say that.'

Toni giggled.

'God! I'm starving too! Let's order quickly.'

The maitre d'hôtel came over. Garry ordered a dozen oysters each with a half bottle of Chablis, followed by the Scotch beef with a baked potato in jacket and a bottle of Batailley 1961. The dessert, it was decided, should be a lemon sorbet.

'Mmmmmm!' Toni purred. 'This job must be marvellous. You do realize this is going to cost a f-o-r-t-u-n-e?'

'So what? I'm worth a fortune.' Under the cover of the table, Garry slid his hand up Toni's mini skirt, but she clamped her legs together.

31

'Mr. Edwards! I'm surprised at you!' she said.

Garry disengaged his hand.

'I'm continually surprising myself, Miss White.'

The oysters arrived.

'Well, tell me ... what is the job?' Toni asked as she cut a fat oyster from its shell. 'God! I adore oysters!'

'Don't be greedy,' Garry said, forking an oyster into his mouth. 'It's never becoming for a young and sexy girl to sound greedy.'

'Shut up! Tell me about the job.'

'Well, it's a dilly. I go to Natal, and as your geography is as dodgy as mine, Natal is somewhere in South Africa. I lug an American photographer around in a helicopter so she can take photos of wild animals. It is a three week assignment and the money is very acceptable.'

Toni's oyster hovered before her mouth. She looked searchingly at Garry who avoided her eyes.

'She? You mean you are flying a *woman* around jungles for three weeks?'

'That's it,' Garry said carelessly. 'Now don't start getting into a state. I've met her. She's around forty-five, looks pregnant, and is the type who slaps you on the back and picks her teeth immediately after a meal.'

Toni stared at him.

'But that sounds horrible.'

'Doesn't it? Still the money is good and after all she could have had a beard and a wooden leg, couldn't she?'

Toni nodded and attacked another oyster.

'Yes, I suppose so.'

There was a long silence while the waiter removed the debris and a longer silence while the beef was served.

Garry stole a look at her face and then grimaced. Hell! he thought, she knows I'm lying. Now what am I going to do?

He said gently, 'Toni, darling, have you got something on your mind?'

'Should I have?' She didn't look at him but concentrated on her beef. 'They have here the most marvellous beef in the world.'

'I wouldn't say in the world. I remember in Hong Kong ...'

'Never mind Hong Kong. Please tell me how much you are being paid to convey a pregnant woman around the jungle.'

'I didn't say she was pregnant, I said she looks pregnant. Not quite the same thing.'

'How much?'

'Three thousand dollars,' Garry lied.

'Well, that's very nice. So you will be away for three weeks?'

'Yes.'

Toni continued to eat. There was a dazed expression in her eyes that began to bother Garry.

'I hear Natal is pretty interesting,' he said. 'It could be quite a trip.'

'Shall we try to enjoy our dinner, Garry? This is the first time I've been to the Rib Room.'

'I thought we were enjoying it. Are you trying to be dramatic?'

Her long lashes flickered at him, then she dug into her baked potato.

'Please let us enjoy something even if we can't enjoy each other.'

That spoilt his meal. Impatiently he pushed aside his plate and lit a cigarette. Toni ate slowly, obviously enjoying the beef. They said nothing until she had finished, then when the waiter had removed the plates, Garry said, 'Just what the hell has suddenly bit you, Toni? This is supposed to be a celebration.'

'I love sorbets. Queen Victoria used to stuff sorbets down the throats of all her over-stuffed guests half-way through the menu. The sorbets allowed them to go on stuffing.'

'I didn't know you were so well educated, darling. I asked what is biting you.'

The lemon sorbets arrived. Garry, in a fit of frustrated rage, crushed his cigarette in the ice.

'Is that how you feel, Mr. Oxfam?' Toni asked, spooning ice into her pretty mouth.

'Look, Toni, I don't know what's come over you, but this has turned into a drag.'

'Has it?' She put down her spoon. 'Garry, dear, I am always asking myself how it is I land up with a lover who lies to me. It is beginning to bore me.'

They stared at each other.

'Women who are able to spot my lies bore me too,' Garry said quietly.

'There it is.' Toni lifted her hands helplessly. 'Damn you, I love you. Let's get out of here and go home and have sex.'

He paid the bill without shuddering with one of the $50 Travellers' Cheques Shalik had given him.

In the taxi, Toni sat away from him, putting her feet up on the tip-up seat.

'This photographer . . . she's marvellous, isn't she?' she asked. 'Darling Garry, don't lie to me . . . tell me.'

He watched the street lights and the rain beating on the pavement, and he sighed. 'Okay . . . yes . . . she's marvellous.'

Toni's small, pretty face tightened with misery.

'Will you be coming back, Garry?'

'Now look, Toni . . .'

'I'm asking you . . . will you be coming back to me?'

He hesitated, thinking of the tawny-haired woman who now filled his mind.

'I don't know.'

'Well, thanks for being truthful.' She moved closer to him and slid into his arms.

Fennel told the taxi driver to take him to the end of Hornsey Road where Jacey had his shabby flat. As the taxi passed Jacey's building, Fennel peered through the rain splashed window, looking for trouble, but saw nothing to alarm him. At the end of the long road, he paid off the taxi and walked back, keeping in the shadows, his eyes alert for trouble.

He reached the entrance of the block, stepped inside and looked at the steep stairs leading to the upper floor of the building, lit by a yellow light bulb.

Instinct warned him he could be walking into danger. He hesitated, then moving silently into the smelly lobby, he stepped into the telephone booth behind the stairs. He dialled Jacey's number. He listened to the steady ringing for some minutes, then he hung up. It was unlikely Jacey would be out in this cold rain at this hour . . . it was after 22.00 hrs. Jacey got up early and went to bed early. Fennel hesitated. His equipment which he had to have for the Natal trip was up there. He had to get it. It was securely hidden in the rafters of Jacey's attic. It would want some finding if they search for it. He hadn't told Jacey where he had hidden it so they would have no success if they had put pressure on Jacey.

He grinned suddenly as an idea came into his mind. He lifted the receiver and dialled 999. To the answering police voice, he said, 'There's bad trouble at 332 Hornsey Road ... top flat ... could be murder,' and he hung up.

He then moved cautiously out of the booth, listened, then walked into the darkness and the rain. Keeping in the shadows, he crossed the road and stood in the entrance of a dark alley to wait.

He didn't have to wait long.

Two police cars came swiftly out of the night, pulled up outside the building and four policemen ran up the steps.

Fennel looked up at Jacey's darkened windows. After a few moments a light flashed up. He waited, leaning against the damp wall of the alley, shivering slightly in the bleak cold. After some twenty minutes, three of the policemen came out, shoving two powerfully built men into the police cars. The two men were handcuffed. They drove away. That left one policeman up there.

What had happened to Jacey? Fennel wondered. Well, he couldn't wait. He had to get his equipment. He took his handkerchief from his pocket and tied it across his face, making a mask, then he crossed the street and entered the building and ran silently up the stairs. When he reached Jacey's floor, he paused to listen. Jacey's front door stood open. He could hear the policeman moving around in the room.

Fennel crept like a ghost to the door and glanced in. The far wall was splashed with blood. His back turned to him, the policeman was kneeling by Jacey's body.

Fennel grimaced. So Jacey, the poor stupid sod, had been carved. He didn't hesitate. Moving swiftly, he was on the policeman before the man realized he was being attacked. With laced fingers, Fennel smashed his hands down on the man's bent neck with one shattering, terrible blow. The policeman spread out over Jacey's blood-stained body.

Fennel darted into the tiny, evil smelling bedroom and up the ladder that led to the attic. In seconds, he had got the bag containing his equipment, then slid down the ladder, out on to the landing. He paused to listen, then went down the stairs to the ground floor, three at the time. Panting, he reached the front door where he paused again, hearing the distant sound of a police siren. He slid out into the rain, ran across the road and backed against the wall of the alley as an ambulance and two police cars came roaring to a standstill.

Fennel grunted . . . well timed, he thought, then set off by the back alleys until he reached a main road. He saw a cruising taxi and waved. The taxi pulled up and he told the driver to take him to the Royal Towers Hotel.

He arrived outside Shalik's suite and rapped on the door. There was a delay, then the door opened. George Sherborn, a portly, elderly man who acted as Shalik's confidential secretary and valet regarded Fennel with startled disapproval. He knew all about Fennel and after hesitating, stood aside and let him in.

'Mr. Shalik is away for the weekend,' he said. 'What is it?'

'I've got to get the hell out of the country fast,' Fennel said wiping his sweating face with the back of his hand. 'I'm in dead trouble. The creeps after me found my pal and carved him. The cops are there now. It won't take them long to find my fingerprints all over the goddamn place, and when they do, I'm blown.'

Sherborn was never flustered. He could rise to any emergency with the calmness of a bishop presiding over a tea party. He knew without Fennel the Borgia ring operation couldn't succeed. He told Fennel to wait and went into the inner room, shutting the door. Half an hour later, he returned.

'A car is waiting for you downstairs to take you to Lydd,' he said. 'You fly by air taxi to Le Touquet. There will be another car at Le Touquet to take you to the Normandy hotel, Paris where you will stay until the Johannesburg plane leaves. Your ticket will be at Orly, waiting for you.' Sherborn's round gooseberry eyes regarded Fennel impersonally. 'You understand the cost of all this will be deducted from your fee?'

'Who says so, fatty?' Fennel snarled.

Sherborn looked at him with contempt.

'Don't be impertinent. Mr. Shalik will be most displeased by what has happened. Now get off.' He handed Fennel a sheet of paper. 'All the necessary details are here for you. You have your passport?'

'Oh, get stuffed!' Fennel snapped and snatching the paper, hurried to the lift.

Five minutes later, seated in a hired Jaguar, he was being whisked down to Lydd.

Chapter Three

Ten minutes after the meeting between Gaye, Garry, Jones and Fennel had broken up, Shalik had come into Natalie's office, an overcoat over his arm and a weekend case in his hand. She paused in her work and looked up.

To Shalik, Natalie Norman was part of his background: useful, exceedingly efficient: a dedicated, colourless woman who had been with him for three years. He had chosen her to be his personal assistant from a short list of highly qualified women an agency had submitted to him.

Natalie Norman was thirty-eight years of age. She spoke fluent French and German, and she had an impressive degree in Economics. With no apparent interests outside Shalik's office she was, to him, a machine who worked efficiently and who was essential to him.

Shalik liked sensual, beautiful women. To him, Natalie Norman with her plain looks, her pallid complexion was merely a robot. When he spoke to her, he seldom looked at her.

'I shall be away for the weekend, Miss Norman,' he said, pausing at her desk. 'I will ask you to come in tomorrow for an hour to see to the mail, then take the weekend off. I have a meeting on Monday morning at 09.00 hrs.,' and he was gone.

There was no look, no smile and not even a 'nice weekend'.

The following morning, she arrived at her usual time, dealt with the mail and was beginning to clear her desk as George Sherborn came in.

She loathed Sherborn as he loathed her. To her thinking, he was a boot-licking, sensual, fat old horror. On the day she began to work for Shalik, Sherborn, his fat face flushed, had run his hand over her corsetted buttocks as she was sealing a large envelope full of legal documents. His touch revolted her. She had spun around and slashed his fat face with the side of the envelope, making his nose bleed.

From then on they hated each other, but had worked together, both ably serving Shalik.

'Have you finished?' Sherborn asked pompously. 'If you have, get off. I'm staying here.'

'I'll be going in a few minutes,' she returned, not looking at him.

Sherborn nodded, regarded her contemptuously and returned to Shalik's office.

Natalie sat for a long moment listening, then when she heard Sherborn dialling a number, she took from a drawer a big plastic shopping bag. From another drawer she took out the tiny tape recorder and three reels of tape. These she hurriedly put in the shopping bag and zipped it shut. She could hear Sherborn talking on the telephone. She moved silently to the door and listened.

'I've got the place to myself, baby,' Sherborn was saying. 'Yes ... the whole week-end. Suppose you come over? We could have fun.'

Natalie grimaced with disgust and moved away. She put on her coat, tied a black scarf around her head and taking the shopping bag, she crossed to the lift and pressed the call button.

As she waited, Sherborn appeared in the doorway.

'You off?'

'Yes.'

She stared bleakly as she saw him looking curiously at the shopping bag.

'Taking all the secrets with you?'

'Yes.'

The lift doors swung open and she entered. As the doors closed, Sherborn smiled sneeringly at her.

Natalie took a taxi back to her two room flat in Church Street, Kensington. She had slept very little the previous night, tossing and turning, trying to make up her mind whether to betray Shalik or not. Even now as she unlocked the front door and entered the small but pleasant living-room which she had furnished with care, she still hadn't made up her mind.

She put down the shopping bag, took off her head scarf and coat and then dropped into an armchair. She sat there for some minutes, knowing she would do it and loathing herself. She looked at her watch. The time was 11.10 hrs. There was always the chance that Burnett wouldn't be at the bank on this Saturday morning. If he wasn't, then it would be a sign for her not to do what she was planning to do. For a brief moment, she hesitated, then crossed to the telephone and dialled a number.

She sat on the arm of the chair as she listened to the ringing tone.

An impersonal voice said, 'This is the National Bank of Natal.'

'Could I speak to Mr. Charles Burnett, please?'

'Who is calling?'

'Miss Norman . . . Mr. Burnett knows me.'

'One moment.'

There was a brief delay, then a rich, fruity baritone voice came over the line.

'Miss Norman? Delighted . . . how are you?'

She shivered, hesitated, then forced herself to say, 'I would like to see you, Mr. Burnett . . . it's urgent.'

'Of course. If you could come at once . . . I am leaving in an hour for the country.'

'No!' Hysterical self-loathing now had her in its grip. 'In half an hour . . . here . . . at my flat! 35a Church Street, fourth floor. I said it was urgent!'

There was a pause, then the rich baritone voice, sounding slightly shocked, said, 'I'm afraid that is not convenient, Miss Norman.'

'Here! In half an hour!' Natalie cried, her voice going shrill and she slammed down the receiver.

She slid down into the seat of the chair, resting her head against the cushion. Her body shuddered and jerked as she began to sob hysterically. For some minutes she allowed herself the luxury of crying. The hot tears finally ran no more. Trembling, she went into the bathroom and bathed her face, then spent some minutes repairing her make-up.

She returned to the sitting-room, opened a cupboard and took out the bottle of whisky she kept for Daz. She poured herself a stiff drink and swallowed it neat, shuddering.

She sat down to wait.

Thirty-five minutes later, the front door bell rang. At the sound of the bell, blood rushed into her face and then receded leaving her face chalk white. For a long moment, she sat motionless, then when the bell rang again, she forced herself to her feet and opened the door.

Charles Burnett, Chairman of the National Bank of Natal, swept into the room like a galleon in full sail. He was a large, heavily-built man with a purple red face, shrewd hard eyes and his bald head, fringed by glossy white hair, was glistening pink. Immaculately dressed in a Savile Row grey lounge suit with a blood red carnation in his button hole, he looked a movie version of what a rich, influential banker should be.

'My dear Miss Norman,' he said, 'what is all the urgency about?'

He regarded her, his mind registering distaste, but he was far too shrewd and experienced to show it. What a dreadful hag! he was thinking: nice figure, good legs, of course, but that pallid face, the plainness of it, those depressing black eyes and the dark overshadowed face.

Natalie had control of herself now. The whisky had given her false confidence.

'Sit down, please, Mr. Burnett. I won't be wasting your time. I have information regarding Mr. Kahlenberg that you will wish to hear.'

Burnett lowered his bulk into an armchair. His expression showed mild interest, but his shrewd mind was thinking: So it has paid off. One drops a seed here and there, and sometimes it germinates.

As Chairman of the National Bank of Natal which was owned by Max Kahlenberg, Burnett was under instructions from his Chief to collect every scrap of information circulating in London that could effect Kahlenberg's kingdom in Natal.

Some twelve days ago, Kahlenberg had sent him a brief cable: *Need information regarding activities of Armo Shalik. K.*

Burnett knew all about Armo Shalik, but nothing of his business activities. The cable dismayed him. To get information about Shalik ... the kind of information that would interest Kahlenberg ... would be as difficult as getting information from the Sphinx. However, Burnett knew he had to do something about this request. When Kahlenberg asked for information, he expected to get it no matter the difficulties or the cost.

It so happened that two days later, Shalik threw a cocktail party in his suite to which Burnett was invited. Here, he met Natalie Norman.

Burnett believed in being pleasant to the underlings. Didn't George Bernard Shaw say once: you may kick an old man: you know what he is, but never kick a young man: you don't know what he will become?

Seeing Natalie supervising the drinks and being ignored by the chattering guests, he had detached himself from his tiresome wife and cornered her. He had charm, and was an easy conversationalist and he quickly learned that this pale-faced, plain-looking woman was Shalik's personal assistant, and he could see that she was sexually starved.

He easily won her confidence and chatted with her for some minutes while his mind worked swiftly. She could be vitally important to him and he knew he couldn't remain with her for long as Shalik was already glancing in their direction with lifted eyebrows.

'Miss Norman,' he said quietly, 'I am in the position to help people like yourself should you need help. Please remember my name; Charles Burnett, the National Bank of Natal. Should you ever get dissatisfied with your job here, should you wish to earn more money, do please contact me.'

As her expression became bewildered, he smiled and left her.

After returning home, he sat in his study and considered his next move. He hoped he hadn't rushed his fences with this pale-faced woman. She could be the spy he needed. Obviously, she needed physical contact with a virile man. Burnett knew all the signs: her thinness, her dark ringed eyes, her depressed expression. What she needed was a lusty bedmate: he decided this must be the first move to ensnare her.

Burnett had many useful contacts and among them was ex-Inspector Tom Parkins of the C.I.D. He telephoned him.

'Parkins ... I am looking for a young rogue who could do a special job for me. He must be completely unscrupulous and good looking with personality and around twenty-five, not older. Do you know of anyone like that?'

The cop voice said, 'Shouldn't be too difficult, sir. Would the pay be interesting?'

'Very.'

'I'll turn it over in my mind, sir. Suppose I call you after lunch?'

'Do that,' Burnett said, satisfied that he would get what he wanted.

Around 15.00 hrs., Parkins telephoned.

'I've got your man, sir,' he said. 'Daz Jackson: twenty-four years of age, excellent appearance, plays a guitar in a fifth rate Soho club and needs money. He served two years for petty larceny three years ago.'

Burnett hesitated.

'This might be a little tricky, Parkins. I'm not letting myself in for blackmail?'

'Oh no, sir. Anything like that ... and it won't happen, I assure you ... I could handle for you. I have quite a lot on this young tearaway. You don't have to worry about that angle.'

'Very well. Send him here at 17.00 hrs. I'll arrange to have ten pounds credited to your account with us, Parkins.'

'That's very kind of you, sir. You will be quite satisfied with Jackson.'

Daz Jackson arrived ten minutes after the hour. He was ushered into Burnett's vast office by Burnett's secretary. She had worked so long for Burnett that nothing surprised her ... not even Daz Jackson.

Burnett regarded the young man as he lounged into the big room, a supercilious grin on his face. He wore mustard-coloured hipsters, a dark-blue frilled shirt and a gilt chain around his neck from which hung a small bell that tinkled as he moved.

What a specimen Burnett thought, but, at least, he is clean.

Without being asked, Jackson lowered his lean frame into a chair, crossed one leg over the other and regarded Burnett with an insolent lift of his eyebrow.

'The ex-bogey said you had a job. What's the pay?' he asked. 'And listen, I don't dig to work in this graveyard. Catch?'

Burnett was used to dealing with all kinds of people and he was adaptable. Although he would have liked to have kicked this young beatnik out, he saw he could be the man he was looking for.

'I'm not asking you to work here Mr. Jackson,' he said. 'I have a special job which you could handle and which pays well.'

Jackson raised a languid hand in mock protest.

'Skip the mister and all that jazz,' he said. 'Call me Daz.'

Burnett's insincere smile became a little stiff.

'Certainly ... but why Daz?'

'The chicks call me that ... I dazzle them.'

'Splendid.' Burnett leaned back in his executive chair. 'What I want you to do is this ...' He explained.

Daz Jackson lolled in his chair and listened. His ice grey eyes searched Burnett's face while Burnett talked. Finally, when Burnett said, 'Well, that's it ... do you think you can handle it for me?' Daz grimaced.

'Let's get it nice and straight,' he said, stretching out his long legs. 'This piece wants to be laid . . . right?' When Burnett

nodded, he went on, 'Once I've given it to her, she'll want more
... right?' Again Burnett nodded. 'Then she has to pay for it ... ₁
you want me to squeeze her dry ... right,'

'Yes ... that is the situation.'

'You will pay me a hundred nicker for doing the job and what
I get out of her I keep ... right?'

Burnett inclined his head. Dealing with a man like this made
him feel slightly soiled.

Jackson leaned back in his chair and stared at Burnett.

'Well, for God's sake, and they call me delinquent!'

Burnett's eyes turned frosty.

'Do you want the job or don't you?'

They stared at each other for a long moment, then Daz
shrugged.

'Oh sure ... what have I to lose? What's this piece like?'

'Plain but adequate,' Burnett returned, unconsciously using
the phrase in the Michelin Guide to France to describe a third
rate hotel.

'Okay, so where do I find her?'

Burnett gave him Natalie's home and business addresses typed
on a blank card.

'I want quick action.'

Daz grinned.

'If you say she's thirsting for it, she'll have it and once she has
had it from me, she'll want it again and again.' Daz regarded
Burnett, his eyes calculating. 'The cops won't come into this?'

'There's no question of that.'

'Well, if they do, I'll squeal. I'm not mad about this job.'

Burnett stared coldly at him.

'But you will do it?'

Daz shrugged.

'I said I would, didn't I?'

'Get as much money out of her as you can. I want her to be in
an impossible financial position. I want her to be up to her eyes in
debt.'

Daz dragged himself to his feet.

'How about some money now ... I'm skint.'

'When you deliver,' Burnett said curtly and waved a dismissal.

In the bitter cold of a January night, Natalie Norman found

her rear off-side tyre was flat. She had been working late, and was now looking forward to getting home and into a hot bath. She had parked her Austin-Mini, as she always did in a cul-de-sac off Park Lane. She stood shivering in the biting wind while she looked helplessly at the flat tyre, when out of the shadows, came a tall, lean young man, wearing a lamb skin lined short coat, his hands thrust deeply into the pockets of his black hipsters.

Daz had learned where Natalie parked her car, and he had let the air out of the tyre some fifty minutes ago. He had stood in a nearby doorway, freezing and cursing until he saw her come to the car. This was his first glimpse of her. He brightened considerably as the street light lit up her long, slim legs. The least he had expected was some woman with legs that could support a grand piano.

He waited, watching her. She moved into the full light and he grimaced. Good body, but so obviously a plain, sex-starved spinster with as much personality as a drowned cat.

Boy! he thought. Will I have to use my imagination to get her laid!

'You in trouble, miss?' he said. 'Can I give you a hand?'

Natalie was startled by his sudden appearance. She looked helplessly to right and left, but there was no one in the cul-de-sac except themselves.

'I have a puncture,' she said nervously. 'It's all right. I'll get a taxi . . . thank you.'

He moved under the street light so she could see him. They regarded each other, and she felt her heart beat quicken. He was lean and tall and like a beautiful young animal, she thought. His hair, curling to his collar, excited her. She felt a rush of blood through her: something that often happened when she saw really masculine men on the street, but her pale, expressionless face revealed nothing of the feeling that was moving through her body.

'I'll fix it,' Daz said. 'You get in the car, miss. Get out of the cold. Phew! It's cold, isn't it?'

'Yes . . . but please don't bother. I'll take a taxi.'

'Hop in . . . I'll fix it . . . won't take me a jiff.'

She unlocked the car door and got gratefully into the little car, closing the door. She watched his movements. He was very quick. Under ten minutes, he came to the car window, wiping his hands on the seat of his hipsters.

'All fixed, miss . . . you can get off.'

She looked up at him through the open car window. He leaned forward, staring down at her. Was there something of promise in his young eyes? she wondered. Her heart was jumping about like freshly landed trout.

'Can't I give you a lift?'

She smiled and when she smiled, he decided she wasn't all that bad to look at.

'You wouldn't be going near Knightsbridge?' he asked, knowing that was where she lived.

'Oh yes . . . Church Street.'

'Well, a lift would be nice.'

He went around the car and slid in beside her. His shoulder touched her and she felt as if she had received an electric shock.

She was furious with herself because her hand was shaking so violently she couldn't get the key into the ignition lock.

'You're cold. Like me to drive, miss?'

Silently, she handed him the keys and he slid out of the car as she moved over to the passenger's seat. Her skirt got rucked up on the gear lever. She hesitated, then knowing her legs and slim thighs were her only attractive features, she let her skirt remain as it was.

'I'm frozen,' she forced herself to say as Daz got under the driving wheel.

'Me too . . . it's perishing.'

She expected him to drive fast and flashily, but he didn't. He drove well, keeping just under the 30 m.p.h. limit and with expert confidence that surprised her.

'Do you live in Knightsbridge?' she ventured.

'Who . . . me?' He laughed. 'Nothing so posh. I live in a rat hole in Parson's Green. I'm out of work. Whenever I get down to my last quid I like to walk around Knightsbridge and window shop. I imagine what I would buy from Harrods if I had a mass of lolly.'

She looked at his handsome profile, and again she experienced this devastating pang of desire.

'But why are you out of work?' she asked. 'People need never be out of work these days.'

'I've been ill. I've got a weak lung . . . plays up sometimes . . . then I get laid off. I've been laid off now for two weeks.' Daz

45

thought: The lies I can tell. I almost believe this myself. Then feeling he was laying it on a little too thick, he added, 'I'll get something next week, I'm feeling fine now.'

Natalie digested all this.

'I'm glad.'

He turned and gave her a smile that had earned him his nick name. She felt sloppily weak as her desire for him mounted.

'You don't have to worry about me, miss. No one, including me, worries about me.' He paused, then went on, 'You're out late, aren't you?'

'I often work late.'

'Church Street you said?'

They were now driving by Knightsbridge Underground Station.

'Yes.'

'You live on your own?'

Oh yes, Natalie thought bitterly. Alone . . . always alone.

'Yes.'

Daz's eyes moved to her legs, exposed to above the knee. Poor cow! he thought. This is going to be easy.

'Well, lots of people live on their own,' he said. 'When they get back from work, they shut themselves in their dreary rooms and that's it until they go out to work the next morning. That's why I like to walk the streets at night. Staying in my room on my own gives me the horrors.'

'I can understand that.' Then as he began to drive up Church Street, she went on, 'This is the place . . . on the right.'

Well here's the crunch, he thought. Is she going to invite me in?

'You mean this big block here?'

'Yes. You go down the ramp to the garage.' She hesitated then said in a small voice, 'I expect you would like a wash after changing that tyre. I think you deserve a drink too.'

He hid a grin. He had felt it would be easy, but not quite this easy.

'Yes. I could do with a wash,' and he drove the car down into the big lighted garage.

They went up in the lift to the fourth floor. Neither of them looked at each other on the way up nor spoke.

She unlocked her front door and led him into the small, bright sitting-room.

'Do take your coat off.' Her voice was very unsteady.

He looked around.

'This is real nice.'

She came to know *nice* was his favourite word.

'The bathroom's through there.'

She left him in the bathroom and she took off her coat and scarf, feeling desire for him raging through her. She was still standing in the middle of the room, white and shaking, when he came out of the bathroom. He knew at once there would be no trouble.

'We don't know each other. I'm Daz Jackson.'

'I'm Natalie Norman.'

'Nice name . . . Natalie . . . I dig for that.'

They stared at each other, then he moved close to her and slid his arms around her.

She shivered as his hands moved down her thin back. For one brief moment, her subconscious mechanism fought to repulse him, but her need was too strong.

She was only dimly aware of being carried into the bedroom. She relaxed on the bed moving a little from side to side as he stripped off her clothes. Then she gave herself up to his animal lust.

Daz Jackson opened his eyes and let out a long, slow sigh. Well, for shouting aloud! he thought as he looked up at the white ceiling. Who would have believed it. It's the best I've ever had!

He turned on his side and looked at Natalie who lay on her back, her hands covering her small breasts, sleeping. He regarded her body. Good, pity about that face. He gave her a gentle prod in the ribs.

'Wake up! I'm hungry. You got any food?'

She stirred and looked up at him, her eyes glazed with a satisfaction she had never known before. She felt as if a hidden door she had long been searching for had suddenly opened and the sun and the breeze and the sound of the sea had come into the barren, dark cave in which she had lived for so long.

'Food . . . of course.' She sat up, swung her legs off the bed and snatched up a wrap. 'Stay there . . . I'll get you something. Would you like a drink . . . I have only gin.'

He regarded her. Her anxiety to please, the soft look in her eyes and her eager trembling made her a bore.

47

'Just grub.'

She ran into the kitchen. He waited a moment, then got off the bed and struggled into his clothes. He saw by the bedside clock that the time was 02.25 hrs. He listened, smelling bacon frying, then he looked around the small neat room. He looked beyond the doorway, across the sitting-room and saw her standing by the stove in the kitchen, her back to him. Working quickly, he went through her chest of drawers. In the top drawer he found a gold cigarette case, a gold lighter and a small jewel box which contained a string of pearls and two rings of little value, but he took all of them, dropping them into his pocket. Then he lounged into the sitting-room and stood in the kitchen doorway.

'Smells nice,' he said.

She turned and smiled at him.

'Can you eat more than four eggs?'

'That'll be fine.'

She hurried past him and quickly laid the table.

'Aren't you eating?' he asked, seeing she had set only one place.

'No . . . it's ready. Sit down.'

He ate hungrily. Well, she certainly could cook eggs and bacon, he thought as he sipped the tea she had poured him. Pity there weren't chips and tomato ketchup, but you can't expect everything.

He was aware of her, sitting on the settee, watching him. There was that soft look in her eyes that told him she was hooked. When he had finished, he sat back, wiping his mouth on the paper serviette she had provided.

'Nice,' he said. 'Really nice.'

'You were hungry, weren't you?'

He stared directly at her.

'Yes . . . and so were you.'

Blood stained her face and she looked away.

'Nothing to turn hot about.' He smiled his dazzling smile. 'It's nature. You liked it, didn't you? I'll tell you something: you were good . . . really good.'

'Please don't talk about it. I've never done it before.'

'So what? You have to start sometime.' He got to his feet.

'Well, I must be taking off.' He paused. 'Thanks for everything. It was real nice . . . all of it.'

He watched her hands turn into fists.

'Wouldn't you like to – to stay?' she said breathlessly. 'It's such a horrid night. You can stay if you like.'

He shook his head.

'Got to get back to my pad.' He began to move slowly to the front door.

'I suppose we – we could see each other again,' she said, her dark eyes desperate.

Here it is, he thought, The hook.

'You never know. Things happen, don't they? So long,' and before she realized he was really going, he had gone.

The front door slammed. The sound was like a disastrous clap of thunder inside her head.

It wasn't until the following evening that she discovered the loss of her cigarette case and lighter, given to her by Shalik as a birthday present, and her pieces of jewellery. The discovery shocked her and she knew at once who had taken them. Her first reaction was to rush to the telephone to inform the police, but then she controlled her anger and sat down to think. He was out of work. He had been hungry. What did she need with a gold cigarette case or the lighter? She didn't smoke anyway. Thinking of him, she decided that he could have everything she owned so long as he came back to her.

For five long, shattering days, she waited with growing desperation to hear from him again until finally a slow horror began to build up inside her that she would have to face the crushing fact that he had made use of her, stolen her things and had forgotten her.

Then on the fifth night, as she sat miserably alone in her flat, facing yet another long night of loneliness, the telephone bell rang. Her heart gave a great leap as she sprang to her feet and ran across the room to snatch up the receiver.

'Yes?'

'This is Daz . . . remember me?'

Her legs felt so weak she had to sit down.

'Of course.'

'Look, I'm sorry I took your things. You mad at me?'

'No . . . of course not.'

'Well, it wasn't nice. I pawned them. I had to have money fast . . . bit of trouble. I'll let you have the tickets . . . Shall I bring them round now?'

'Yes.'

'Okay, then,' and then line went dead.

He didn't arrive until 22.05 hrs., giving her a frantic wait of an hour and a half. She thought he looked thinner and he wore a scowling frown that gave him a dark, sullen look.

'Here you are,' he said, dropping three pawn tickets on the table. 'I shouldn't have done it . . . but I was in trouble . . . I had to raise money fast.'

'It's all right. I understand. Are you hungry?'

'No . . . I can't stay. I've got to go,' and he turned to the front door.

She gazed at him in panic.

'But you – please stay. I want you to stay.'

He turned on her, his eyes suddenly savage.

'I've got to raise more money,' he said. 'I can't fool around here. There's a girl living near my pad who is trying to raise something for me. I've got to see her tonight.'

'A girl?' Natalie turned cold. 'Daz . . . won't you explain what this is all about? Won't you sit down? I could help you if you would explain.'

'I've had enough out of you.' Daz shook his head. 'Anyway, Lola has practically promised . . .'

'Please sit down and tell me.'

He sat down. It was easy to lie to her. The horse that was a cinch. The bet he couldn't cover, and now the bookie was after him.

'They are a tough lot,' he concluded. 'If I don't raise fifty pounds by tomorrow they are going to do me.'

'*Do* you?' Natalie looked at him in horror. 'What does that mean?'

'Carve me, of course,' he said impatiently. 'Slash me with a razor . . . what do you think?'

She imagined that handsome face bleeding. The thought made her feel faint.

'I can let you have fifty pounds, Daz . . . of course.'

'I can't take it from you . . . no, I'll see Lola.'

'Don't be silly. I'll give you a cheque now.'

An hour later, they were lying side by side on the bed. Natalie was relaxed and happy for the first time since last she had seen Daz. It had been wonderful, she was thinking, better even than the first time. She turned to look at Daz and her heart contracted to see that sullen dark look back on his face again.

'What is it, Daz?'

'Just thinking . . . can't a man think, for God's sake?'

She flinched at the harsh note in his voice.

'Wasn't it good for you? Did I disappoint you?'

'I wasn't thinking about that.' He looked impatiently at her in the shaded light of the bedside lamp. 'That's over. I'm thinking ahead. Just shut up a minute, will you?'

She remained still, waiting and watching his hard young face and the way his eyes shifted, reminding her of an animal in a trap.

'Yes,' he said finally as if speaking his thoughts aloud. 'That's what I'll do. I'll get out. I'll go to Dublin. That's it! Danny will get me a job.'

Natalie sat up, clutching the sheet to her breasts.

'Dublin? What do you mean?'

He frowned at her as if just aware she was with him.

'What I say. I have to get out. That fifty quid you've given me will keep Isaacs off my neck for a couple of days. By then, I'll be out of his reach.'

She felt as if she were going to faint again. Watching her, Daz saw he had played a trump card.

'But you said if I gave you the money it would be all right,' she gasped. 'Daz! Tell me! What do you mean?'

He looked scornfully at her.

'You don't imagine a bookie would carve anyone for fifty quid, do you? I'm in the hole for twelve hundred.'

Once she had absorbed the shock, her trained mind searched for ways and means. Twelve hundred pounds! It was an impossible sum! She had taken an expensive autumn vacation, and she had only two hundred pounds to her credit at her bank. But the idea of Daz leaving England and going to Ireland was unthinkable.

She slid off the bed and put on her wrap while Daz watched her. He saw there was a change of expression on her face. He saw her mind was working, and he lay still, waiting results. He wondered uneasily if he had put the price too high, but Burnett had told him to clean her out. Just suppose she hadn't the money?

She walked around the room while she thought, then she came and sat on the bed, looking straight at him.

'Daz . . . if I give you twelve hundred pounds, could you remain in London?'

'Of course, but you can't give me that amount . . . so why talk about it?'

'I can try. How long can you wait?'

'Why talk about it?' He lay on his back, staring up at the ceiling. 'I must get out. I'll go tomorrow.'

'How long can you wait?' Her voice was now as harsh as his.

'Ten days . . . not more.'

'If I give you this money, Daz, will you come and live here?'

How easy it was to lie to this poor cow, Daz thought.

'You mean move in? You want me here?'

'Yes.' She tried to control her voice. 'I want you here.'

'It would be nice . . . yes, of course. I could get a job, and we could be together. But why talk about it?'

'I think I can manage,' Natalie threw off her wrap. She dropped down beside him on the bed. 'You love me, don't you, Daz?'

That old jazz, he thought and pulled her to him.

'You know I do. I'm crazy about you.'

'Then love me!'

While Daz slept by her side, Natalie lay staring into the darkness, her mind busy. She knew it would be hopeless to ask Shalik to lend her a thousand pounds. Even as she was telling Daz that she thought she could get the money for him, she had been thinking of Charles Burnett of the National Bank of Natal.

Natalie was well aware of the espionage and counter-espionage that goes on in present day big business. She knew Burnett had been hinting that he would pay for information and she had treated the hint with the contempt it had deserved but now under pressure with the real risk of losing Daz forever, she found she was much less scrupulous.

Before dozing off, she made up her mind to contact Burnett.

Leaving Daz sleeping, she had gone to the Royal Towers hotel the following morning.

She quickly arranged Shalik's mail on his desk, left a note to remind him of his various engagements for the day and then returned to her office.

At this hour, she knew Shalik was being shaved and dressed by the hateful Sherborn. She hesitated only briefly, then called the National Bank of Natal.

She was put through immediately to Charles Burnett who had

already been alerted by Daz by telephone what to expect.

'Of course, Miss Norman. I will be delighted to meet you again. When would it be convenient?'

'At your office at 13.15 hrs.,' Natalie told him.

'Then I will expect you.'

When she arrived, Burnett greeted her like a benign uncle. Natalie told him abruptly that she needed one thousand pounds.

'It is a large sum,' Burnett said, studying his pink finger nails, 'but not impossible.' He looked up, his eyes no longer benign. 'You are an intelligent woman, Miss Norman. I don't have to spell it out to you. You want money: I want information concerning Mr. Shalik's activities that might have the remotest reference to Mr. Max Kahlenberg of Natal.'

Natalie stiffened.

During the past few days she had learned from scribbled notes on Shalik's desk and from overhearing him talk to Sherborn that something important was being planned that concerned a man named Max Kahlenberg who until this moment had meant nothing to her.

All Shalik's private correspondence was typed by Sherborn. Natalie's job was to arrange Shalik's appointments, his lunches and dinners and to act as hostess at his cocktail parties as well as taking care of the hundred and one personal matters that made his life smooth and easy.

'I don't think I can help there,' she said, dismay in her voice. 'I'm excluded from Mr. Shalik's business life, but I do know something is going on to do with a man called Kahlenberg.'

Burnett smiled.

'I can help you, Miss Norman. Your task will be absurdly easy. Let me explain . . .'

Twenty minutes later, she accepted a plastic shopping bag he had ready which contained a miniature tape-recorder, six reels of tape and a very special eavesdropping microphone.

'The quality of the recordings, Miss Norman, will naturally influence the amount of money I will pay you. However, if you are urgently in need of a thousand pounds and providing you give me something of interest, the money will be available.'

Now, after eight days, he was here in her flat, his fat, purple face creased in a smile, his blood red carnation a status symbol.

'My dear Miss Norman, what is all the urgency about?'

During the past three days, Burnett's microphone had eaves-
dropped.

During the past eight days Daz had slept with her, sweeping
her into a world of technicolor eroticism. She had promised him
the money and he was prepared to service her, telling himself
that in the dark, all cats were grey.

'I have information regarding Mr. Kahlenberg which you will
wish to hear,' Natalie said. The whisky she had drunk made her
feel reckless and light headed.

'Splendid.' Burnett crossed one fat leg over the other. 'Let me
hear it.'

'Mr. Shalik is arranging to steal the Caesar Borgia ring from
Mr. Kahlenberg,' Natalie said. 'I have three tapes, recording the
details of the operation and who are involved.'

'The Borgia ring?' Burnett was surprised. 'So he is after that?
My congratulations, Miss Norman. Play me the tapes.'

She shook her head.

'I want one thousand pounds in ten pound notes before you
hear the tapes, Mr. Burnett.'

His smile became fixed.

'Now, Miss Norman, that won't do. How do I know you even
have the tapes? I must hear them . . . let us be reasonable.'

She had the tape-recorder already loaded and she let him listen
to three minutes conversation between Shalik and Garry
Edwards, then as Shalik was saying, 'All that will be explained
tonight. You will not be alone. The risks and responsibilities will
be shared,' she pressed the stop button.

'But nothing so far has been said about Mr. Kahlenberg,' Burnett pointed out, looking hungrily at the tape recorder.

'When you have brought me the money, you will hear the rest,
but not before.'

They regarded each other and Burnett saw it would be useless
to try to persuade her. He got to his feet, reminding himself that
one thousand pounds meant as much to Max Kahlenberg as one
penny meant to the Prime Minister of England.

Two hours later, his Saturday afternoon ruined, Burnett was
back with the money. He listened to the tapes, his fat, purple face
becoming more and more startled. He realized as he listened that
he was getting these tapes cheaply.

'Splendid, Miss Norman,' he said as she wound off the last
tape. 'Really splendid. You have certainly earned your fee. Any

further information you can get like that I will, of course, pay you as handsomely.'

'There won't be a next time,' Natalie said. Her face was white and her expression of self-loathing startled Burnett. She thrust the tiny tape recorder at him. 'Take it away!'

'Now, Miss Norman . . .'

'Take it! Take it!' she screamed and fearing a scene, Burnett grabbed the recorder and the three tapes and hurriedly left. It was only on his way down in the lift that he realized she hadn't returned the expensive eavesdropping microphone. He wondered if he should go back for it, but her distraught face and the wild look in her eyes warned him not to. He would pick up the microphone after the week-end when she would be calmer.

Some three hours later, Daz returned to the flat. He had already checked with Burnett who had told him the money was waiting for him.

Elated that he was going to lay his hands on such a sum, he had dated a chick to meet him at Billy Walker's Boozer that was once an elegant restaurant and from there they would go to a club in King's Road and from there into her bed.

He was through with Natalie. With a thousand pounds in hand and with his know-how, Dublin would be the place for him.

He was slightly startled when he entered the flat to find Natalie sitting on the settee, white faced, trembling and crying.

'What the hell's up?' he demanded, thinking how ugly she looked.

She dabbed her eyes and straightened.

'I have the money, Daz.'

He moved further into the room.

'You have? What are you so miserable about? You oughta be pleased.'

'Judas wasn't pleased . . . he hanged himself.'

Daz had vaguely heard of Judas. He wasn't sure who he was, but he had an idea he was a baddie and not a goodie.

'What are you talking about? Who's hanging who?'

'Nothing . . . you wouldn't understand. Are you hungry?'

He wiped his mouth with the back of his hand.

'Where's the money?'

'You're not hungry? I've bought you a steak.'

'To hell with the steak. Where's the money?'

Looking at him, she was shocked to see the greed on the lean, handsome face.

She got unsteadily to her feet and went to a cupboard. She brought the money to him in neat stacks.

It made her heart contract to watch him fondle the money. This couldn't be the man she loved so desperately who had opened the hidden door in her life: this was a greedy, vicious young animal who mauled the money as he had mauled her body.

'Are you pleased?'

He ignored her and began stuffing the money into his various pockets.

'What are you doing?' Her voice went shrill.

He stowed away the last packet of money and then regarded her.

'Getting the hell out of here ... that's what I'm doing.'

'You mean now you have the money, you – you don't want me?'

'Who the hell would want you?' He pointed a finger at her. 'I'm going to give you some advice. From now on, baby, keep your legs tightly crossed. That's your trouble. You dig your own grave,' and he was gone.

Natalie stood motionless, her hand against her slow thumping heart. She listened to the lift descend, taking him out of her life forever.

Then she walked slowly to a chair and sat down. She remained there as the hands of the clock on the wall moved around its face, marking the hours. Then when the light began to fade she eased her stiffness by stretching out her long, slim legs. Her mind began to work again. After all, she told herself, why should he care? I could have guessed what was going to happen. She closed her eyes. Now her lack of charm and her plainness was underlined as it had never before been so underlined. She realized all along she had been praying, waiting, hoping for a miracle, but this wasn't the year of miracles.

She thought of the long, lonely nights ahead of her. She knew too that her conscience would be burdened by the guilt of her betrayal. She had done this disgusting act of disloyalty only to keep Daz for herself. Why go on? She asked herself. You can't hope to live with yourself ... so why go on?

She went into the kitchen, moving slowly like a sleepwalker.

and found a small, sharp vegetable knife. Taking this with her, she paused to put the front door on the latch, then she went into the bathroom. She turned on the bath taps and stood in a black daze until the bath was half full of tepid water. She kicked off her shoes and stepped into the bath. Her pleated skirt ballooned out and she pressed it down. She felt the comforting water soak through her clothes to her despairing body.

She lay still. Would it hurt? They said it was the easiest way to die. Gritting her teeth, she drew the sharp blade across her left wrist. She cut deeply and she fought back a cry of pain. The knife slipped from her hand. For a brief moment, she looked at the water surrounding her, now turning pink and darkening, then she closed her eyes.

She lay there, thinking of Daz with his handsome face and his long black curly hair and his beautiful strong body until she quietly slid away from a life she no longer had use for.

Chapter Four

Armo Shalik returned to his suite at 08.30 hrs. on Monday morning. He was met by Sherborn who reported that Fennel was in Paris. He explained the circumstances while Shalik sat at his desk, glowering at him.

'I hope I did right, sir. Had I know where to contact you, I would, of course, have consulted you.'

The fact that Shalik had had an unsatisfactory week-end with a call girl somewhere in the country, and he had no intention of advertising this fact to Sherborn, increased his rage.

'Well, he's gone. He said nothing about what he thought of the Kahlenberg set-up?'

'No, sir. He was in and out like a rocket.'

Shalik had a feeling this was going to be a black Monday. Had he known that the three tapes, recording the details of his plan to steal the Borgia ring had already arrived on Max Kahlenberg's desk, he would have considered this Monday to be a disaster, but he didn't know.

Irritated and short tempered, he presided over the 09.30 hr. meeting, explaining to Gaye, Garry and Ken Jones that Fennel had had to leave and was now in Paris.

'There is no need to go into details,' he said. 'Mr. Fennel left so hurriedly he was unable to tell me his opinion about Kahlenberg's security measures. I trust he will be able to tell you when you all meet at the Rand International hotel. As I have a busy morning, there is no useful purpose served in prolonging this meeting.' He looked at Garry. 'You have studied the maps I gave you?'

'Yes . . . no trouble,' Garry said. 'I'll get there.'

'Well, then the operation is now in your hands. I have done my best to make it easy for you. It is now up to you. You will be leaving tonight, and you will arrive at Johannesburg tomorrow morning.' He paused, hesitated, then went on, 'It is only fair to warn you that Fennel is a dangerous criminal, but absolutely necessary if this operation is to succeed.' He looked directly at Garry. 'You appear able to take care of yourself, so I will ask you also to take care of Miss Desmond.'

'That will be my pleasure,' Garry said quietly.

'Oh, Armo!' Gaye said impatiently. 'You know I can well look after myself. What are you fussing about?'

'Men fuss over beautiful women. I am no exception,' Shalik said, lifting his fat shoulders. Again he looked directly at Garry who nodded. 'Well, bon voyage and success, Sherborn will give you your tickets and all the necessary details.'

When the three had gone, Shalik looked for his list of appointments which Natalie always left on his desk. He couldn't find it. Again, he had a feeling that this Monday was going to be more than tiresome. Angrily, he went into her room. That she was not sitting at her desk as she had always sat for the past three years startled him. He looked at his watch. The time was 10.00 hrs. Returning to his office, he rang for Sherborn.

'Where is Miss Norman?'

'I have no idea, sir,' Sherborn returned indifferently.

Shalik glared at him.

'Then find out! She may be ill. Call her flat!'

The buzzer of the telephone sounded. Impatiently, Shalik waved to Sherborn to take the call.

Sherborn picked up the receiver and said in his pompous voice, 'Mr. Shalik's residence.' There was a pause, then in a voice suddenly off-key, he said, 'Who? What did you say?'

Shalik looked angrily at him, then stiffened for Sherborn had lost colour and there was alarm in his eyes.

'Hold on.'

'What is it?'

'Sergeant Goodyard of the Special Branch is asking to speak to you, sir.'

The two men looked at each other. Shalik's mind flew to those three dangerous currency transactions he had recently made when he had moved some nine hundred thousand pounds out of England. Could Scotland Yard have possibly got on to that? He felt his hands turn moist.

Steadying his voice and not looking at Sherborn, he said, 'Tell him to come up.'

Three minutes later, Sherborn opened the door of the suite to be confronted by a large, heavily-built man with probing eyes, a mouth like a fly trap and a jaw like the prow of a ship.

'Come in, sir,' Sherborn said, stepping aside. 'Mr. Shalik will see you immediately.'

Sergeant Goodyard moved into the room. He stared at Sherborn, then lifted heavy eyebrows.

'Why, hello George . . . I thought you were dead.'

'No, sir,' Sherborn said, sweat on his face.

'A pity. You keeping out of trouble?'

'Yes, sir.'

Sergeant Goodyard surveyed the outer room with a critical eye.

'You've found a nice little nest here, haven't you, George? Better than Pentonville I dare say.'

'Yes, sir.'

Sherborn opened the door to Shalik's office.

After staring at him for a long moment, Goodyard walked into the impressively luxurious room.

Shalik glanced up. He regarded the police officer as he came slowly to the desk.

'Sergeant Goodyard?'

'Yes, sir.'

Shalik waved him to a chair.

'Sit down, sergeant. What is it?'

Goodyard settled himself in the chair and looked stonily at Shalik who felt the unease that all guilty people feel when under police scrutiny, although his face remained expressionless.

'I believe Miss Natalie Norman works for you?'

Surprised, Shalik nodded.

'That is right. She hasn't come in this morning. Has something happened to her?'

'She died Saturday night,' Goodyard told him in his flat, cop voice. 'Suicide.'

Shalik flinched. He had a horror of death. For some moments he remained motionless, then his quick, callous mind became alive. Who was he going to find to replace her? Who was now going to look after him? The fact that she was dead meant nothing to him. The fact that he had relied on her for the past three years to arrange his social and business life meant a lot.

'I'm sorry to hear that.' He reached for a cigar and paused to clip the end. 'Was there any reason?'

What a bastard! Goodyard thought, but his cop face revealed none of his disgust.

'That is why I am here, sir. I hoped you could tell me.'

Shalik lit the cigar and let the rich smelling smoke roll out of his mouth. He shook his head.

'I'm sorry, but I know nothing about Miss Norman ... nothing at all. I have always found her an efficient worker. She has been with me for three years.' He leaned back in his executive chair and looked directly at Goodyard. 'I am a busy man, Sergeant. It is impossible for me to take much – if any – interest in the people who work for me.'

Goodyard felt in his overcoat pocket and produced a small object which he laid in front of Shalik on the white blotter.

'Would you know what that is, sir?'

Shalik frowned at the thick paper clip: the kind that is used to clip together heavy legal documents.

'Obviously a paper clip,' he said, curtly. 'I hope you have reason for asking me such a question, Sergeant. You are taking up my valuable time.'

'Oh, yes, I have a reason,' Goodyard was unperturbed by Shalik's sharp note. 'I understand, Mr. Shalik, that you are engaged in many transactions about which rival companies could be interested.'

Shalik's face hardened.

'Surely that is no business of yours?'

'No, sir, but it could explain this object here,' and Goodyard tapped the paper clip.

'Just what do you mean?'

'This apparent paper clip is a highly sensitive microphone which is illegal to possess and which is used only by authorized bodies. In other words, sir, this gadget is only used in espionage work.'

Shalik stared at the paper clip, feeling a sudden rush of cold blood up his spine.

'I don't understand,' he said.

'This paper clip was found in Miss Norman's flat,' Goodyard explained. 'Fortunately the district detective investigating her death was smart enough to recognize what it was. It was passed to the special branch. That is why I am here.'

Shalik licked his dry lips as he said, 'I know nothing about it.'

'Have you seen it before?'

'I don't think so ... how can I tell?' Controlling a feeling of panic, Shalik waved to a pile of documents on his desk, each held together with big paper clips, but none quite as big as the clip lying on his blotter. 'It is possible ... I don't know.'

'To use this microphone successfully,' Goodyard said, picking up the microphone and putting it in his pocket, 'a special tape-recorder is required. Could I examine Miss Norman's desk?'

'Of course.' Shalik got to his feet and led the way into Natalie's office. 'That is her desk.'

Goodyard's search was quick and thorough. He also looked into the many filing cabinets and into the closet where Natalie used to hang her coat.

'No ...' He turned to Shalik. 'Have you any reason to believe that Miss Norman was spying on you?'

'Certainly not.'

'You know nothing about her private life? I understand she had a young man living with her. Several people in her building have seen him entering her flat. Would you know who he is?'

Shalik's face showed his astonishment.

'I can scarcely believe that ... still, if you say so. No, I know nothing about her.'

'Further inquiries will be made, sir. I shall want to see you again.'

'I am usually here.'

Goodyard made for the door, then paused.

'I don't know if you are aware that your servant is George Sherborn who has served six years for forgery.'

Shalik's face was expressionless.

'Yes, I know. Sherborn is a reformed character. I am very satisfied with him.'

Goodyard's bleak, cop eyes stared at him.

'Do they ever reform?' he asked and left.

Shalik sat down at his desk. He took out his handkerchief and wiped his damp hands while he thought.

Had the microphone ever been on his desk?

Suppose it had? Had that white faced bitch been recording his transactions? He thought of the dangerous currency deals. Then there was the information given him by the P.A. to the Chancellor of the Exchequer which had netted four of his clients fortunes. There was the merger leak he had got from a typist frantic for money. The list was endless. If she had planted the microphone on his desk, how many of his deals had been taped? There was also the Kahlenberg affair. Had she recorded that? He screwed his handkerchief into a ball, his face vicious. Where was the tape-recorder? Maybe, he thought, someone had got at her and she had only been half-convinced. Maybe, he thought, she had taken the microphone and had second thoughts about taking the tape-recorder. She could have felt soiled. She was a neurotic type. Maybe she had decided to kill herself rather than to betray him. But, suppose she had recorded the conversation he had had with the four who were going after the Borgia ring? Suppose the tapes were already on their way to Kahlenberg?

He leaned back in his chair, staring at the opposite wall while his mind worked swiftly.

Should he warn them?

He considered the risk. The three men were expendable. He would be sorry to lose Gaye Desmond. He had taken a lot of trouble to find her, but, after all, he told himself, Gaye wasn't the only woman in the world. If he did warn them that the operation might already be blown, wouldn't they back out? His fee for regaining the ring was to be $500,000 plus expenses. He grimaced. It was too large a sum to give up because of four people. In a situation like this, he told himself, he must keep his nerve and gamble that this dead bitch hadn't recorded what was said.

After more thought, he decided to say nothing and to wait.

He reached for his mail and because he had a trained mind, a few minutes later, he had completely dismissed Goodyard's visit and had dismissed the thought that Kahlenberg could know that he was to lose the Borgia ring.

Charles Burnett sailed majestically into his office. He had lunched well on smoked salmon and duck in orange sauce and was feeling well fed and satisfied with himself.

His secretary handed him a coded cable, telling him it had arrived a few minutes ago.

'Thank you, Miss Morris,' Burnett said, stifling a small belch. 'I'll attend to it.'

He sat down at his desk and unlocked a drawer. From it he took Kahlenberg's code book. A few minutes later, he was reading:

Pleased. Visitors will receive exceptionally warm welcome. Have bought 20,000 Honeywell for your Swiss account. K.

Burnett asked Miss Morris to give him the day's quotation on Honeywell. She told him the share had moved up three points.

Burnett was feeling extremely satisfied when ex-Inspector Parkins came on the line.

'I thought you should know, sir, that Mr. Shalik's secretary, Natalie Norman, was found dead in her flat this morning ... suicide.'

Burnett was unable to speak for some seconds.

'Are you there, sir?'

He pulled himself together. So he had been right: she had looked mental: he had been sure of it.

'Why should you imagine, Parkins, that I could be interested?' he asked, trying to keep the quaver out of his voice.

'Well, sir, this young tearaway, Daz Jackson was seeing a lot of her. I thought possibly you should be told, but if I have made a mistake, then I apologize.'

Burnett drew in a deep, slow breath.

'So Jackson visited her ... very odd. Will he be involved?'

'I doubt it. Jackson left for Dublin on Saturday night. The police do have his description. Still, Dublin is a good place for him to be.'

'Yes. Well, thank you, Parkins ... interesting.' Burnett could almost see Parkins' foxy face and the expectant hope in his little eyes. 'There will be an additional credit in your account,' and he hung up.

He sat for a long moment, thinking. He remembered the expensive microphone left in Natalie's flat. For some seconds, he worried about it, then he assured himself no one would recognize it and it would be thrown away with her other rubbish.

Parkins' call, however, had spoilt his afternoon.

The lobby of the Rand International hotel was crowded with large, noisy American tourists who had just arrived off a bus from which assorted luggage was already spewing.

Wrapped in transparent raincovers, they milled around, shouting to each other, completely oblivious to the uproar they were creating. The lobby was shattered by cries of: 'Joe ... you seen my bag?' 'Goddamn this rain ... where's the sun?' 'For God's sake, Martha, you're only exciting yourself. The luggage isn't all out yet.' 'Hey, Momma ... the guy wants our passports!' and so on and so on. America had taken over the Rand International for some ear splitting moments while the white and the coloured staff coped with the invasion.

Sitting near the breakfast-room with a view of all this commotion, Lew Fennel watched sourly.

Rain fell steadily. The Bantus, sheltering under umbrellas, paused to stare through the glass doors of the hotel at the confusion going on in the lobby. Having stared, they grinned and moved on, splay footed, the men in shabby European dress, the women wearing bright scarves over their heads and bright dresses that set off their colour.

Fennel sucked at his cigarette and watched the last of the American party, still screaming to each other, whisked away in the lifts. He had been in Johannesburg now for thirty-six hours. He had had a nervous half day in Paris before catching the plane to South Africa. Now, for the first time for over a month, he felt relaxed and safe. Moroni and the police were far away.

He looked at his watch, then shifted his heavy body more comfortably in the chair.

A black Cadillac drew up outside the hotel and Fennel got to his feet as he saw Gaye's tawny head emerge as she ran under the cover of the hotel's canopy.

Ten minutes later, the three were with him in the small sitting-room of his suite on the eighth floor of the hotel.

Fennel was in an amiable and expansive mood.

'I guess you all want to rest,' he said as he served drinks from the refrigerator, 'but before you go, I'd like to fill you in with what we can expect . . . okay?'

Garry eased his heavy shoulders. The fourteen hour flight had cramped his muscles. He looked at Gaye.

'Do you want to listen or do we take a bath first?'

'We listen,' Gaye said, leaning back on the settee. She took a sip of the gin and tonic Fennel had given her. 'I'm not all that dead.'

Fennel's eyes narrowed. So Edwards was already taking a proprietory interest in the woman he had mentally reserved for himself.

'Well, make up your minds!' he said, his temper rising. 'Do you or don't you want to hear?'

'I said yes,' Gaye said, her cool eyes surveying him. 'What is it?'

'Those invoices Shalik gave me. It puts us right in the photo.' Fennel drank a little of his whisky and water. 'I now know the museum must be underground. A lift complete with all the works was delivered to Kahlenberg's place and as the house is on one floor, the answer to the lift is the museum is under the house. Get it?'

'Keep going,' Garry said.

'Listed in the invoices are six television close-circuit sets and one monitor. That tells me there are six rooms in the museum and there is one guard watching the monitor, probably somewhere in the house. By pressing buttons, the guard can survey each of the six rooms, but only one at the time.' Fennel lit a cigarette, then went on, 'I know this system. The weakness is that the guard could fall asleep, he could read a book without watching the monitor or he could leave to go to the toilet. But we must find out if he does all or any of these things and if he is on duty at night. That's your job to find out,' and Fennel pointed his stubby finger at Garry.

Garry nodded.

'The door to the museum is listed on the invoice. It is of massive steel. I worked for Bahlstrom so I know about their equipment. The door has a time lock on it. You set it at a certain time and set the counter dial at another time and no one on earth except Bahlstroms can open the door between these two times.'

Fennel grinned. 'Except me. I know how to handle that time lock. I helped to build it. Now we come to something you will have to take care of.' He was talking directly at Garry.

'The lift . . . this is a tricky one. We will do the job at night. What I want to know is if the lift is out of action during the night. By that, I mean is the electricity cut. If the lift doesn't work at night I don't see how the hell we are getting to the museum.'

'Let's be pessimistic,' Garry said. 'Suppose the juice is cut off?'

'It's up to you to turn it on or we're sunk.'

Garry grimaced.

'There's always the chance there could be stairs as well as the lift.'

'Could be.' Fennel nodded. 'That too you have to find out. It's your job to find out as much as you can once you're in. Another thing you will have to tell me is how I get in . . . door or window? Again this is up to you. All the dope you collect you give to me over the two-way radio so I'll know what to be ready for.'

'If the dope can be got, I'll get it.'

Fennel finished his drink.

'If you don't get it, we don't do the job . . . it's as simple as that.'

Gaye got to her feet. She looked sensationally lovely in the sky blue cotton dress she was wearing: a dress that clung to her figure. The three men watched her.

'Well, I'll leave you and take a tub. I want some sleep. I didn't sleep a wink on the plane.'

She nodded to them and left the room. Garry stretched and yawned.

'Me too . . . unless you want me for anything else?'

'No.' Fennel looked at Ken. 'How about the equipment? Have you got that lined up?'

'I think so. I'll take a bath and go check. A friend of mine is organizing it for me. I sent him a cable from London telling him what we want. I'll go over there and see how far he's got. Do you want to come with me?'

'Why not? Okay, I'll wait here for you.'

Garry and Ken went along the corridor to their rooms. They were all on the eighth floor: each had a small suite with an air conditioner and a view of the city.

'Well, see you,' Garry said, pausing at his door. 'This could be a tricky one.'

Ken grinned. Garry had now learned that Ken was an incurable optimist.

'You never know . . . could work out fine. Me for the tub,' and he went off whistling to his room.

An hour later, he returned to Fennel's room. Fennel had been punishing the whisky and looked a little flushed.

'Shall we go?' Ken asked, leaning against the doorway.

'Yeah.' Fennel got to his feet and the two men walked along the corridor to the lifts.

'This pal of mine runs a garage on Plein Street,' Ken said as the lift descended. 'It's just across the way. We can walk.'

They pushed their way through another consignment of American tourists who had just arrived. The noise they were making made both men wince.

'What makes an American so noisy?' Ken asked good humouredly. 'Do they imagine everyone around is stone deaf?'

Fennel grunted.

'I wouldn't know. Maybe they weren't taught as kids to keep their goddamn traps shut.'

They paused under the canopy of the hotel and surveyed the rain sweeping Bree Street.

'If it's going to rain like this in the Drakensberg Range we're in for a hell of a time,' Ken said, turning up his jacket collar. 'Come on . . . may as well start getting wet . . . it'll be good practice.'

Their heads bent against the driving rain, the two men walked briskly across to Plein Street.

Sam Jefferson, the owner of the garage, a tall, thin elderly man with a pleasant, freckled face greeted them.

'Hi Ken! Had a good trip?'

Ken said the trip was fine and introduced Fennel. Jefferson lost some of his sunny smile as he shook hands. He was obviously a little startled at the cold, hard expression on Fennel's face. Fennel wasn't his kind of people.

'I got all the stuff and it's there laid out for you,' he went on turning to Ken. 'Take a look. If there's anything I've forgotten, let me know. Excuse me now. I've got a gear box in my hair.' Nodding, he went off across the big garage to where two Bantus were staring vacantly at a jacked up Pontiac.

Ken led the way to a small, inner garage where a Land Rover

was parked. A Bantu, sitting on his haunches and scratching his ankle got slowly to his feet and gave Ken a wide, white toothy grin.

'All okay, boss,' he said, and Ken shook hands with him.

'This is Joe,' he said to Fennel. 'Sam and he have collected all the stuff we need.'

Fennel had no time for coloured people. He glowered at the smiling Bantu, grunted and turned away. There was an awkward pause, then Ken said, 'Well, Joe, let's see what you've got.'

The Bantu crossed to the Land Rover and pulled off the tarpaulin that covered the bonnet. 'I got it fixed like you said, boss.'

Welded to the front of the radiator was a drum between two steel supports. Around the drum was wound a long length of thin steel cable. Ken examined it, then nodded his satisfaction.

'What the hell's that for?' Fennel demanded, regarding the drum.

'It's a winch,' Ken explained. 'We're going over some very sticky roads and we could easily get bogged down. When there's heavy rain, the roads over the Drakensberg can be hell. This winch will drag us out without us breaking our backs.' He found a small yacht anchor lying on the floor of the Land Rover. 'See this? We get stuck, and all we have to do is to slam this anchor into a tree root and winch ourselves out.'

'The roads going to be that bad?'

'Brother! You have no idea. We have quite a trip ahead of us.'

Fennel scowled.

'Those other two have it the easy way . . . flying in, huh?'

'I don't know so much about that. If one of the fans falls off, they land in the jungle and that will be that. I'd rather drive than fly in this country.'

'Boss . . .' Joe, still smiling, but uncomfortable in Fennel's presence, pulled off a tarpaulin that covered a long trestle table standing away from the Land Rover. 'You want to check this stuff?'

The two men moved over to the equipment laid out. There were four jerrycans for water, another five for gas, four sleeping bags, four powerful electric torches with spare batteries, two six foot steel perforated strips for getting out of mud, a collapsible tent, two wooden cases and a large carton.

'With luck, I reckon we'll take five days in and four days out to do the job,' Ken said, patting the two wooden cases. 'We have enough canned food to last us that time.' He tapped the carton. 'That's booze: four Scotch, two gin and twenty-four quarts of beer. I have a Springfield, a 12 bore and a .22. There's plenty of game where we are going. You like guinea-fowl? Impala? Ever tried a saddle of Impala done over a slow fire and served with Chilli sauce?' He grinned and rolled his eyes. 'It's marvellous!'

'How about medical supplies?' Fennel asked.

'In the Land Rover . . . complete medical chest. I took a safari first-aid course a while ago. I can handle anything from a snake bite to a broken leg.'

'Looks like you've taken care of it all.' Fennel lit a cigarette and let smoke drift down his nostrils. 'Then all we have to take is our own personal kit?'

'That's it . . . we travel light . . . just a change.'

'I've got my tool bag.' Fennel rested his fat back against the Land Rover. 'It's heavy, but I can't do without it.'

'Well, so long as you can haul it.'

Fennel cocked his head on one side.

'We drive, don't we?'

'We might have to walk some of the way. Even with this winch the road up to Kahlenberg's place could sink us and if it does, we walk.'

'How about taking the nigger along?'

'Look, friend, drop that.' Ken's face had hardened. 'We don't talk about niggers here. We talk about natives. Bantus or non-Europeans but not niggers.'

'Who the hell cares?'

'I do, and if we're going to get along, you will care too.'

Fennel hesitated then shrugged.

'Okay, okay, so what? What's wrong with taking the native, the Bantu, the non-European bastard along with us to carry the goddamn bag?'

Ken regarded him, his dislike plain.

'No. He could talk his head off when he gets back. I've a friend of mine who's joining us at our camp at Mainville. He worked with me when I was on a game reserve. He's coming with us. He is a Kikuyu and a marvellous tracker. Without him, we would never get there. He's out at Kahlenberg's estate now finding a way through the guards and let me tell you there are around three hundred Zulus guarding the estate, but I'll bet when we meet at Mainville, he'll have found a way through them, but he doesn't carry anyone's stuff but his own. Just get that into your skull.'

Fennel squinted at him through his cigarette smoke.

'What is he ... black?'

'He is a Kikuyu ... that makes him coloured.'

'A friend?'

'One of my best friends.' Ken stared hard at Fennel. 'If that's so difficult for you to believe let me tell you the Bantus out here are damn good friends when you get to know them and damn good people.'

Fennel shrugged.

'This is your country ... not mine. Suppose we go back to the hotel? This goddamn rain is giving me a thirst.'

'You go on. I've got to settle up for all this stuff and get it loaded. Suppose we all have dinner together? There's a good restaurant next to the hotel. We can iron out anything that needs ironing out. We could get off tomorrow.'

'Okay ... see you,' and Fennel left the garage and headed for the hotel.

Ken watched him go, frowning. Then shrugging, he moved over to where Sam Jefferson was working on the Pontiac.

They all met at the Checkmate restaurant which is part of the Rand International Hotel a little after 20.30 hrs. As was her privilege, Gaye was the last to arrive, wearing a lemon-coloured cotton dress and making every male eye in the restaurant stare at her with that hungry look males have for really beautiful women.

Fennel eyed her as she slid into her chair and felt sweat break out down his fat back. He had known many women in his life, but none to compare with her. He felt a white hot surge of desire go through him and it so shook him that he purposely dropped his serviette so he could bend, grope for it while he forced the desire out of his face.

'Well, what are we going to eat?' Garry asked.

They were all hungry and chose sea food on the broche and breaded veal with french fry.

'How's it been going?' Garry asked Ken. He was aware of Fennel's tenseness and glanced at his flushed face, then looked away.

'All under control. We have everything organized now. We could leave tomorrow if that suits you two.'

'Why not?' Garry looked at Gaye for confirmation and she nodded.

'The sooner we're off, the easier for us it will be. The rains have started. There is a chance the rain hasn't reached Drakensberg yet, but if it has, Fennel and I will have quite a trip. So, if it's all right with you, we will leave at o8.oo hrs. tomorrow morning. We drive in the Land Rover ... it won't be too comfortable as we're pretty loaded. We have around three hundred kilometres to our camp at Mainville.' The sea food was served and when the waiter had gone away, Ken went on, 'Mainville is about four hundred kilometres from Kahlenberg's place. The chopper will be at Mainville. The airlift won't take long unless anything goes wrong. You two will stay in camp for a day while Fennel and I go on by road. Then you take off. We'll be in touch with you on the two-way radio. I've tested them ... they're good. We'll reach Mainville just after noon with luck. Fennel and I will start around o5.oo hrs. the following morning. You will take off around 10.oo hrs. the following morning. You should arrive at Kahlenberg's place in an hour or so. You don't want to be too early. How does it sound?'

'Sounds fine,' Garry said. 'And the chopper? How about service and gas?'

'All that's taken care of. You'll have enough gas to take her in and bring her out. I have a guarantee she will be fully serviced. It's up to you to satisfy yourself she is okay, of course, but from what I've been told, she'll be there waiting for you and ready to go.'

'What's Mainville like?' Gaye asked, laying down her knife and fork.

Ken grinned. 'A horse and buggy town. I have the camp organized five miles out of town in the bush.'

They began eating the veal which they enjoyed. They discussed further details of the operation. Both Gaye and Garry were aware that Fennel had little to say except to grunt over his food and keep looking at Gaye. At the end of the meal, they had coffee while Ken talked. He was an easy and interesting talker and he amused them.

'You'll have fun driving to Mainville,' he said. 'I won't be going on the highway on the last lap and you'll see game ...

warthogs, Impala, waterbuck, vervet monkeys and so on. I'll give you the dope on them when we see them if you're interested. I was once a game warden on a swank reserve ... taking people around in a Land Rover to spot game.'

'What made you give it up?' Gaye asked. 'I should have thought it was a lovely life.'

Ken laughed.

'You would, wouldn't you? Nothing the matter with the animals, but the clients finally got me down. You can't expect to go into the bush and just find animals waiting for you. You have to be patient. There are days, especially in this season, when you can drive for miles without seeing a thing. The clients always gripe ... blaming me. After a couple of years I got fed up with it. There was one client who really bore down on me. Okay, he had no luck. It was the rainy season, and he wanted to photograph a buffalo. He had a thousand dollar bet with a pal back in the States that he would bring the photo back ... no buffaloes. We drove for hours hunting for them, but no luck, so he took it out on me.' Ken grinned. 'I hauled off and busted his jaw ... got eighteen months in jail for it so when I came out, I quit.'

Fennel who had been listening impatiently, broke in, 'Well, I don't know what you two guys are going to do, but I'm inviting Miss Desmond to come along with me and take a look at the nightspots.' He stared directly at Gaye, his face set. 'How about it?'

There was a slight pause. Garry looked quickly at Fennel's flushed face and then at Gaye who smiled, completely relaxed.

'That is nice of you, Mr. Fennel, but excuse me. If I'm going to get up so early, I need my sleep.' She got to her feet. 'Good night. See you all in the morning,' and she made her way, followed by male stares, out of the restaurant.

Fennel sat back in his chair, his face pale, his eyes burning.

'Some brush-off,' he snarled. 'Who the hell does she think she is?'

Ken got to his feet.

'I'll fix the bill and then I'm going to bed,' and he walked over to the cash desk.

Garry said quietly, 'Take it easy. The girl's tired. If you want to go somewhere I'll come with you.'

Fennel didn't appear to hear. He sat there, his eyes slightly mad, his face now getting back some colour. He got heavily to his feet and walked out of the restaurant and to the lift. He was shaking with frustrated rage.

All right, you bitch, he was thinking as the lift doors swung open. I'll fix you! Just let me get you alone for ten minutes and I'll fix you so goddamn fast you won't know what's hit you.

He reached his room, slammed the door shut and tore off his clothes. He threw himself down on the bed, his nails biting into the palms of his hands, sweat running down his heavy jowls.

For more than an hour, his lewd mind enacted the things he would do to her when he had her alone, but after a while, the erotic thoughts became exhausted and his mind began to return to normal.

He suddenly remembered what Shalik had said: *You will leave Gaye Desmond strictly alone ... try something like that with Miss Desmond and I promise you Interpol will receive your dossier from me.*

How had Shalik found out about the three killings?

Fennel moved uneasily on the bed. He reached for a cigarette, lit it and stared across the room, lit by the revolving sign across the way.

He was suddenly back in Hong Kong, coming off a junk at Wanchai's Fenwick Street pier. He had been on a smuggling trip with three of his Chinese friends. They had unloaded a cargo of opium at Chu Lu Kok Island without any trouble and Fennel had $3,000 in his hip pocket. He was due to fly back to England in ten hours. After being cooped up in the stinking junk for six days, he was in need of a woman.

His Chinese friends had told him where to go. He had walked along Gloucester Road amid rickshaws, the fast moving traffic, the fruit vendors and the crowds of noisy Chinese until he had come to the brothel, recommended.

The Chinese girl was small, compact with heavy buttocks which Fennel liked, but she was as animated as a side of beef. She acted merely as a receptacle for his lust and when the unsatisfactory union was over, Fennel, with half a bottle of whisky inside him, dulling his senses, slept, but Fennel only ever slept slightly below the level of unconsciousness. He had always led a dangerous life and had trained himself never to become entirely unconscious, no matter how much he drank. He came awake to find the girl, still naked, her ivory skin lighted by the street light coming through the uncurtained window, helping herself from his well stuffed wallet.

Fennel was off the bed and had hit her before he was fully awake. His fist smashed into her face, snapping her head back and she went down, his money falling from her small hand, her eyes rolling back.

Fennel snarled at her, then began to collect the money. It was only when he had thrown on his clothes and had stuffed his wallet into his hip pocket that he realized something was wrong. He bent over the still body and a chill crawled up his spine. He lifted her head by her thick hair and grimaced as the head rolled horribly on the shoulders. His savage, violent blow had broken her neck.

He looked at his watch. He had two hours before he took off for London. He left the room, shutting the door and walked down the stairs to where an old Chinaman was seated at the desk to check clients in and out. He knew he would have to pay for his freedom.

'I'm leaving by junk in twenty minutes,' he lied. 'The whore's dead. What's it going to cost?'

The yellow wrinkled face showed nothing: a parchment map of old age.

'One thousand dollars,' the old man said. 'I have to call the police in an hour.'

Fennel showed his teeth in a savage snarl.

'Old man, I could wring your neck . . . that's too much.'

The Chinaman lifted his shoulders.

'Then five hundred dollars and I call the police in half an hour.'

Fennel gave him the thousand dollars. He had been in Hong Kong long enough to know a bargain was a bargain. He had to have at least an hour to get clear and he had got clear.

Lying in his bed, watching the reflected light making patterns on the opposite wall, he remembered the girl. If she had been more responsive, he wouldn't have hit her so hard. Well, he told himself without conviction, she had deserved what she had got.

The male prostitute he had been unlucky enough to run into in a dirty, evil smelling alley in Istanbul, also got what he deserved. Fennel had come off a ship to spend a few hours in the city before going on to Marseilles. He had brought three kilos of gold from India for a man who was paying well: á fat, elderly Turk who wanted the gold as a bribe. Fennel had done the deal, collected the money and then found a girl to spend the night with. Thinking about her now, Fennel realized she had been smart. She had got him drunk and when the time came for them to share the hotel bed, he had been too drunk to bother with her. He had slept three hours, waking to find her gone, but at least she hadn't been a thief. Livid with frustrated rage, and nearly sober, Fennel had started back to his ship. Here, in this sleazy alley, he had met a perfumed boy: handsome with liquid black eyes and a sly, insinuating smile, who had importuned him. Fennel had vented his rage on him, smashing his head against the wall, leaving a big red stain where the wall had been dirty white.

A woman, peering out of her window, had seen the act of brutal violence and had begun to scream. Fennel got back to his ship, but it was only when the ship sailed that he considered himself safe.

Fennel often lived with his ghosts. He kept telling himself that the dead had no part in his life, but they persisted in his mind. In moments like this, when he was sexually frustrated, and alone, his past violence kept on intruding.

This third murder haunted him more than the other two. He had been hired by a wealthy Egyptian to open a safe belonging to a merchant to whom the Egyptian had given bonds as security for a big loan. Fennel understood these bonds were forgeries and they could be discovered at any moment: the job was urgent.

He had got into the palatial house easily enough and had settled down in front of the safe to open it. The time was 02.45 hrs. and the household was asleep.

The safe was old-fashioned and Fennel had trouble in opening it. As he finally got the safe door open, his tools scattered around him, the door leading into the room where he was pushed open.

Fennel snapped off his torch, grabbed up a short steel bar with which he had been working and spun around.

A shadowy figure stood in the doorway, then the light went on.

A girl stood in front of Fennel in a nightdress and dressing-gown. She was small, dark with large black eyes and an olive complexion. She could not have been older than ten years of age – in fact she was nine. She stared at Fennel in terror and her mouth began to open to scream. He reached her in two swift strides and slammed the steel bar down on her head.

In that moment of panic, he had had no hesitation about killing her. The blow, as he well knew, was lethal. She had seen him, and if he had merely stunned her, she could have given the police a description of him.

He had snatched the bonds from the safe, bundled his tools together and had left. It was only when he got into his car that he saw blood on one of his hands and became fully aware of what he had done.

Those big, terrified dark eyes often appeared in his dreams. From the newspapers the following day, he learned the child was a deaf-mute. He had tried to convince himself that she was better dead, but when he was alone and in bed, the picture of the child in her nightdress and the look of terror on her face as she tried to scream pricked at what remained of his conscience.

He lay watching the red and blue light from the sign across the way, reflected on the ceiling until finally, he drifted off into an uneasy sleep.

Chapter Five

Max Kahlenberg always woke at 05.00 hrs. It was as if he had an alarm clock inside his head. During the seven hours in which he slept, he might have died. He had no dreams nor did he stir until he opened his eyes to watch the sun rise over the magnificent range of mountains that lay beyond the huge picture window opposite his bed.

The bed was enormous, set on a dais with a shell-shaped headboard done over in lemon-coloured silk. Within his reach was a set of push-buttons set in fumed oak. Each button controlled his method of rising. The red button opened and closed the lemon-coloured window drapes. The yellow button lowered the bed to the floor level so he could swing himself into his electrically propelled wheel chair. The blue button opened a hatch by his bedside through which his coffee tray came. The black button filled his bath automatically and at exactly the right temperature. The green button operated the TV monitor at the end of his bed, putting him in direct contact with one of his secretaries.

Max Kahlenberg came awake and touched the red button. The window drapes swung open and he viewed the sky, seeing the scurrying clouds and he decided rain couldn't be far off. He switched on the defused light concealed behind the headboard and thumbed the red button. He shifted himself higher in the bed as the hatch at his side slid up and a tray containing a silver coffee pot, a jug of milk, a container of sugar and a cup and saucer slid within his reach and the hatch closed.

Lying in the enormous bed, Max Kahlenberg looked like a handsome movie star. His head was completely shaved. He had wide set, blue-grey eyes, a well-shaped nose and a big, humourless mouth with a thin upper lip. He always slept naked, and as he hoisted himself up, he revealed a deeply tanned, magnificently developed torso.

He drank his coffee, lit a cigarette and then pressed the green button that connected him with one of his secretaries. The TV screen lit up and he saw Miah, an Indian girl, who did the early morning shift, reach for a pencil and pad. He regarded her with pleasure. He liked beautiful women, and made a point only of employing women who pleased his eyes. The girl, her thin dark face classically beautiful, her big eyes looking directly at him although she couldn't see him, said, 'Good morning, sir.'

Kahlenberg studied her, then said, 'Good morning, Miah. Has the mail arrived?'

'It is being sorted now, sir.'

'I'll be ready to dictate in an hour. Have your breakfast,' and he snapped off the set. He then pressed the black button which would fill his bath and lowered the bed to floor level. He threw off the sheet covering him.

At that moment Kahlenberg turned from a fine looking, handsome athlete into a grotesque freak. No one except his mother and his doctor had ever seen his legs. They had never grown from the time he had been born. In comparison to his well developed torso, they were two ghastly looking appendages, perfectly formed, unable to support his weight and which he loathed with a bitterness and revulsion that not only completely spoilt his

77

life but had made him dangerously mentally disturbed.

No one was ever allowed into his bedroom while he was in it himself. It was only when he was dressed and in his chair which had a snap-on cover over his legs that he felt safe from prying eyes.

He hoisted himself into the chair and ran it into the vast bathroom.

An hour later, he emerged, bathed and shaved and having had a thorough work-out in the well-equipped gymnasium that led off the bathroom. He wrapped the lower part of his body in a cotton loin cloth, put on a white open neck shirt, snapped the cover over the chair and steered the chair into the long corridor that led to his office.

Coming towards him was a fully grown cheetah. This was Hindenburg, Kahlenberg's constant companion. He stopped the chair and waited for the big cat to approach him. He rubbed the thick fur while the cat made a deep, throaty sound, then with a final pat, Kahlenberg sent the chair on its way, with Hindenburg following behind, and reaching a pair of double doors which opened automatically, he propelled himself into the room.

Kahlenberg's office was vast with a window that ran the length of the view side of the room.

From his big desk, he had an uninterrupted view of his lawns, the banks of flowers, the distant jungle, the undulating grass covered hills dotted by the scattered rondavels of his Zulus to the Drakensberg Range.

His mail was on his desk marked with various coloured stickers, donating its priority.

Before going to bed, he had made notes of various affairs that needed attention. He pressed the green button on his desk and when the TV monitor lit up and he saw Miah seated at her desk, he began to dictate.

An hour later, he had finished the previous day's notes.

'That is all, Miah. Is Ho-Lu there?'

'She is waiting now, sir.'

'I'll be ready for her in half an hour,' and he switched off the set.

He went rapidly through the mail of some fifty letters, made quick decisions that would add to his already vast fortune, then lit up the monitor screen again.

This time a flower-like Vietnamese girl was at the desk, patiently waiting. He greeted her and began dictating.

By 10.00 hrs. he had cleared his desk. He sat for some moments, relaxing, his fingers caressing Hindenburg's head, then he flicked down a switch on the intercom and said, 'Come in, please.'

There was a moment's delay, then a tap sounded on the door which swung open.

Guilo Tak, Kahlenberg's personal assistant came in, shut the door and approached the desk.

Guilo Tak was a tall, thin man with a mop of jet black hair that emphasized his cadaverous complexion. His black eyes were sunk deep and burned feverishly in his skull-like face. Born of an Italian mother and a Czech father, he had shown astonishing talent for figures at an early age. He had obtained a job in a Swiss bank and quickly proved himself a financial genius. When Kahlenberg had asked one of the directors of the bank if he knew of a man suitable to be his P.A., the director had no hesitation in recommending Tak.

Kahlenberg found him not only a financial genius but utterly ruthless, utterly efficient and utterly loyal. For some considerable time, Kahlenberg had been hiring expert art thieves to supply his museum. Considerable organization and discussions were needed and Kahlenberg begrudged the time. He had hesitated whether to hand these machinations over to Tak, and finally decided after some eighteen months, that Tak could be trusted. Tak was now not only in charge of the museum, but also handled Kahlenberg's portfolio, often making suggestions and pointing to opportunities which Kahlenberg with his other occupations might have missed.

'Good morning, sir,' Tak said with a stiff little bow.

'Sit down,' Kahlenberg said, resting his elbows on his desk and staring at Tak, thinking what an extraordinary looking man this was. 'Any news of the Borgia ring affair?'

'Yes, sir. The three thieves concerned arrived at the Rand International hotel a few minutes ago. Fennel arrived the day before yesterday. He came from Paris. A garage owner, Sam Jefferson, has been buying their equipment. I have a list of it here if you wish to see it. I have also photographs of these people taken as they arrived at the airport.' He paused to give Kahlenberg a quick glance before laying a large envelope he had brought with him on the desk. 'You may find the woman attractive.'

Kahlenberg glanced at the blown-up photographs of the three men and laid them on the blotter but he sat for some moments studying Gaye's photograph. Then he glanced up. 'What do you know about her?'

'All their dossiers are in the envelope, sir.'

'Thank you, Tak. I'll see you later.'

When Tak had gone, Kahlenberg picked up Gaye's photograph and again studied it for several minutes, then he opened a drawer and put the photograph away. He read the four dossiers, studied the list of equipment, read that the camp was situated near Mainville and a helicopter had arrived there the previous day. He put all the papers back into the envelope and locked it away. He sat staring with hooded eyes down at his blotter for a long time, then with a slight nod of satisfaction at the decision he had reached, he set his chair in motion and snapping his fingers at Hindenburg, he propelled himself out into the garden and along the broad path for a half hour's break. The big cat wandered by his side.

Back at his desk at 11.00 hrs., Kahlenberg dealt until lunch time with more papers that had arrived. He lunched on a smoked trout with horseradish sauce and a coffee, then returning to his office, sent for Tak again.

'How much did I pay for the Borgia ring?' he asked.

'Sixty thousand dollars. Mercial paid a quarter of a million. We got it very cheaply. Now Mercial is paying Shalik half a million to recover it. Absurd, but without it, his Borgia collection is spoilt.'

'I am inclined to let him have it back,' Kahlenberg said, staring at Tak who said nothing. He knew by now the way Kahlenberg's mind worked. 'It might be amusing, but it wouldn't do to let these four have it without working for it, would it?'

Tak inclined his head and continued to wait.

'So why not let them arrive here? As you say the woman is attractive. It will be interesting to see if Fennel who is supposed to be such an expert can break into the museum. Let us encourage them. I can leave the details to you.'

'You want them to walk away with the ring, sir?'

'We will make their entrance easy and their exit difficult, but if they can get it off the estate, then I think they would be entitled to keep it, but only if they can get it off the estate.' Kahlenberg's eyes searched Tak's face. 'You understand?'

'Yes, sir.'

'So we let them in and make it difficult for them to get out. If anything should happen to them, I suppose the crocodiles would welcome extra food.'

Tak's eyes narrowed.

'Is it your wish something should happen to them, sir?'

'Well, it would be awkward if they got into the museum and then got away to talk. We wouldn't want Interpol here making inquiries. The Vatican was particularly incensed at losing the bust of Jupiter. How that rogue ever got it out of the Vatican has always puzzled me. No, it wouldn't do for Interpol to know the museum is below ground.'

'But there was some suggestion, sir, that you were returning the ring to Mercial.'

'Yes . . . I will return the ring but not his operators.'

Tak didn't follow this, but he waited.

'Our Zulus would welcome a manhunt for a change, I think?'

'They can be relied on, sir.'

'Yes . . . they are very close still to the savage. That may not be necessary, of course. Our enterprising four could get lost. Still, let them be alerted. Arrange some sort of reward and insist on proof.'

'Yes, sir.'

'I must admit such a hunt would amuse me.' Kahlenberg's thin-lipped mouth tightened. 'When they have been hunted down and the ring returned to me, I will mail it to Mercial.' He rubbed his jaw as he stared at Tak. 'We mustn't make a mistake. It would be dangerous if even one of them got away. What chances do you think they have against a hundred of my Zulus and the jungle?'

Tak considered the problem, then shook his head.

'No chance at all, sir.'

'That's what I think.' Kahlenberg paused, thinking of the photograph locked in his desk. 'Pity about the woman.'

Tak got to his feet.

'Is there anything else, sir?'

'Yes . . . let me have the Borgia ring.'

When Tak had gone, Kahlenberg flicked down a switch on the intercom and said, 'Send Kemosa to me.'

A few minutes later an old, bent Bantu, wearing immaculate

white drill came into the office. Kemosa had served Kahlenberg's father and was now in charge of the native staff, ruling them with a rod of iron. He stood before Kahlenberg, waiting.

'Is the old witch doctor still on the estate?' Kahlenberg asked.

'Yes, master.'

'I never see him. I thought he was dead.'

Kemosa said nothing.

'My father told me this man has great experience with poisons,' Kahlenberg went on. 'Is that correct?'

'Yes, master.'

'Go to him and say I want a slow working poison that will kill a man in twelve hours. Do you think he could supply a poison like that?'

Kemosa nodded.

'Very well. I want it by tomorrow morning. See he is suitably rewarded.'

'Yes, master.' Kemosa inclined his head and went away.

Kahlenberg pulled a legal document towards him and began to study it. A few minutes later Tak came in carrying a small glass box in which, set on a blue velvet support, was the Caesar Borgia ring.

'Leave it with me,' Kahlenberg said without looking up.

Tak placed the box on the desk and withdrew.

After reading the document and laying it down, Kahlenberg picked up the glass box and leaning back in his chair, he slid off the lid and took out the ring.

He took from a drawer a watchmaker's glass and screwed it into his eye. He spent some moments examining the ring before he found the minute sliding trap, covered by a diamond that gave access to the tiny reservoir that held the poison.

They left the Rand International hotel a little after 08.00 hrs. and headed for Harrismith on the N.16 highway.

They were all wearing bush shirts, shorts, knee stockings, stout soled shoes and bush hats around which was a band of cheetah skin. The men all eyed Gaye as she climbed into the front seat of the Land Rover. The outfit set off her figure and suited her. Again Fennel felt a stab of frustrated desire go through him.

Ken Jones took the wheel and Garry and Fennel sat on the rear bench seat. It was a tight squeeze for the four of them and their equipment. Each had brought along a rucksack containing their personal essentials and these were piled on the rear seat between the two men.

The sky was grey and the atmosphere was close and steamy and they were glad when they had left the city and had got on to the open road.

'This is going to be a pretty dull run,' Ken said. 'Two hundred kilometres to Harrismith, then we turn off the National road and head down for Bergville. We'll get to Mainville for lunch, pick up our guide and then we have thirty kilometres through jungle to the camp. That'll be fun: we're certain to see some game.'

'Who's looking after the chopper?' Garry asked, leaning forward. 'You haven't just left it in the jungle, have you?'

Ken laughed.

'I hired four Bantus to guard it. I know them ... they're okay. It only arrived yesterday. You've nothing to worry about.'

Gaye said she was glad to leave Johannesburg.

'I didn't like it.'

'I don't know anyone who does,' Ken returned. 'But you'd like Cape Town and go crazy about Durban.'

The three chatted together as the Land Rover ate up the miles. Garry noticed that Fennel was sullenly silent. He sat forward with his heavy bag of tools between his feet and his little eyes continually eyeing Gaye's back and the view he could get of the side of her face.

Every so often they came upon a series of beehive shaped huts where they could see the Bantus moving aimlessly about, and tiny boys guarding lean, depressed looking cattle and herds of goats.

Gaye asked a stream of questions which Ken answered. Fennel paid no attention to the chatter. All he could think of was to get Gaye alone. He was confident, once he did get her alone, she would submit to him. He had no interest in black people and he wished Ken would stop yakking.

It was after 14.00 hrs. when they drove into Mainville's town centre that consisted of an untidy square, shaded by magnificent flamboyant trees in full flower. To the left of the square was the post office. Next to it was a native store and across the way was a shop run by a Dutchman who seemed to sell everything from a pair of boots to a bottle of cough mixture. The Bantus, sitting under the trees, watched them curiously, and two or three of them waved languidly to Ken who waved back.

'You seem to be a known character around here,' Gaye said.

'Oh, sure. I get around. I like these guys and they remember me.' Ken drove around the square and headed for a large dilapidated garage. He drove straight in.

Two Bantus came over and shook hands with him as he left the Land Rover. Ken spoke to them in Afrikaans and they nodded, beaming.

'Okay, folks,' he said turning to the others. 'We can leave it all here and go to the hotel for lunch. I could eat a buffalo.'

'You mean they won't steal any of this stuff?' Fennel asked.

Ken regarded him, his mouth tightening.

'They're friends of mine . . . so they won't steal any of the stuff.'

Fennel climbed down from the Land Rover.

'Well, if you're sure about that.'

The other three walked out into the blinding sunshine. Since leaving Johannesburg the sun had come out and it was hot.

The hotel was plain but decent and Ken got a good welcome from a fat, sweating Indian who beamed at the other three.

'Seen Themba?' Ken asked as they walked into the big dining-room.

'Yes, Mr. Jones. He's around. Said he would be here in half an hour.'

They all had a good chicken curry lunch, washed down with beer. From their table, they could see across the square to the garage and Fennel kept looking suspiciously at the garage.

'They're not stealing anything!' Ken said sharply. He had become exasperated by Fennel's suspicion. 'Can't you enjoy your lunch, for God's sake?'

Fennel squinted at him.

'The stuff in that tool bag is worth a lot of lolly,' he said. 'It's taken me years to collect. Some of those tools I've made myself. I'm making sure no goddamn blackie steals it.'

Seeing Ken's face flush with anger, Gaye broke in to ask about the hotel. The tension eased a little, then Ken got to his feet.

'I'll fix the bill, then go look for Themba.'

'Is he our guide?' Gaye asked.

'That's right.'

'And another black friend of his,' Fennel said with a sneer.

Ken hesitated, then walked away.

Garry said, 'Wouldn't it be an idea if you tried to be pleasant for a change? Right now, you act as if you have a boil on your ass.'

Fennel glowered at him.

'I act the way I like, and no one stops me!'

'Plenty of time to squabble when the job's done,' Gaye said quietly. 'Be nice, Mr. Fennel.'

He glowered at her, got up and walked out of the restaurant.

Gaye and Garry paused to congratulate the fat Indian on his curry, and then followed Fennel across the square to the garage.

'He's sweet, isn't he?' Gaye said softly.

'He's a fat slob. If he goes on like this, he'll get a poke in his snout!'

'Remember what Armo said . . . he's dangerous.'

Garry scowled.

'So am I. It bothers me that Ken has to travel with him.'

But he was less bothered when he saw a tall, magnificently built Bantu, wearing bush clothes with a bush hat pinned up Australian fashion on one side, shaking hands with Ken.

'That must be Themba. Well, Ken and he can take care of Fennel; that's for sure.'

Ken made the introductions. Whereas Garry and Gaye shook hands, Fennel just stared at the big Bantu and then walked over to the Land Rover to make sure his bag of tools was still there.

'Themba only talks Afrikaans,' Ken explained. 'So conversationally he's a dead loss to you two.'

'I think he looks wonderful,' Gaye said admiringly.

'He's great. We've worked together for five years . . . no better tracker in Natal.'   .

They climbed into the Land Rover. Themba occupied a small swing-out seat at the rear, placing him above the others and giving him a good view of the country.

'Now, we go into the jungle,' Ken said. 'If there's any game to spot, Themba will find it.'

Another ten minutes of driving brought them off the main road to a grit road and the drive became bumpy.

'It gets worse as it goes on,' Ken said cheerfully, 'but you'll get used to it.'

It did get worse, and Ken had to cut down speed. Pot holes began to appear in the road and the Land Rover banged and bumped, making everyone hold on, with Fennel cursing under his breath.

A mile or so further on, Themba said something to Ken, and Ken slowed and steered the Land Rover off the road into the bush. They were moving slowly now and they all had to look out for thorny bushes and low hanging branches which became hazardous as they went on.

Suddenly before them was a big waterbuck with its majestic antlers, looking towards them. It turned and was away with high leaping steps, displaying a perfect ring of white fur around its rump.

'Oh, I love him!' Gaye explained. 'And that white ring ... it's marvellous!'

'Do you know how he got that?' Ken asked, grinning. 'I'll tell you. When the waterbuck arrived at the Ark, he rushed up to Noah and said, "Mr. Noah, please where is the nearest toilet?" Noah said, "You'll have to wait. All the toilets have just been painted." The waterbuck said, "I can't wait." It's had that ring ever since.'

'Why don't you look where you're driving and stop the yak?' Fennel growled while the others laughed.

'Can't please everyone all the time,' Ken said, shrugging, and continued on.

Gaye was noticing that many of the trees were broken and dead, giving the bush a stricken look.

'Did lightning do all this damage?' she asked.

'What, those trees— No ... elephants. Must have had a big herd through here at one time. The elephant is the most destructive beast of any wild game. They strip the trees and smash them as they move. Wherever an elephant has been, you'll find dead trees.'

A little later they came upon five giraffes and Ken stopped within fifty metres of them. The animals stood motionless, staring.

'I wish I hadn't packed my camera,' Gaye sighed. 'They seem completely tame.'

'They're not tame ... they're eaten up with curiosity,' Ken explained, and even as he spoke the gigantic animals turned and lolloped away, covering the ground at high speed although seeming to move like a slow motion film.

'Lions dig for them, but they seldom catch them,' Ken went on, setting the Land Rover moving again.

'Are there any lions in this district?' Gaye asked. 'I'd love to see one.'

'You will, and hear them too.'

Themba from his perch above them was continually calling to Ken, giving him directions.

'Without this guy,' Ken confided to Gaye, 'I'd never find the camp. He has a compass built inside his head.'

After half an hour's drive, during which time they disturbed a large herd of zebras which went crashing away into the thick bush almost before they could be seen, they came out of the bush on to a wide flat clearing where the helicopter was parked.

Squatting before the helicopter were four Bantus who rose to their feet with wide grins as the Land Rover pulled up.

'Here we are,' Ken said getting out of the truck. 'I'll pay these guys off. We don't want them hanging around. Themba and I can get the tent up.'

Garry went at once to the helicopter. Gaye slid to the ground and stretched. It had been a bumpy ride and she felt stiff and hot. Fennel got down and lit a cigarette. He showed no inclination to help Themba unload the equipment, but stood with his hands in his shorts pockets, eyeing Gaye as she stood with her back to him, her legs wide apart, her hands on her hips.

Ken got rid of the Bantus and came back to the Land Rover.

'There's a big pool beyond those trees and a waterfall,' he said to Gaye, pointing. 'It's safe swimming . . . no crocs.'

'Can I help?'

'No, thanks . . . Themba and I can handle it.'

He joined Themba, and together the two men unloaded the tent.

Breathing unsteadily, Fennel moved over to Gaye.

'A waterfall, huh? Suppose we go take a look at it?'

He was expecting her to refuse, and already his vicious temper began to rise. She regarded him, her face expressionless, then to his surprise, she said, 'Yes . . . let's look at it,' and turning, she walked ahead, making for the thick line of trees and high elephant grass that surrounded the clearing.

Fennel felt a hot rush of blood through his body. Was this an invitation? He looked quickly towards the helicopter. Garry was busy stripping off the engine tarpaulin. Ken and Themba were occupied with unfolding the tent. Shaking a little, Fennel strode after Gaye who had now disappeared into the bush.

He caught up with her as she moved along a narrow track and he slowed his pace, his eyes on her slim back and long beautiful legs. Some twenty metres further on they came to a small water-fall that fell some ten metres into a big basin of water which flowed at its far end into a broad stream. The basin formed a perfect, artificial bathing pool.

She turned as he reached her.

'Isn't it lovely?'

The sun beat down on them. They were surrounded by trees. They could have been the only two people on earth.

'Let's have a swim,' Fennel said and stripped off his shirt. 'Come on, baby, strip off.'

She looked at his hairy, muscular torso, her eyes watchful as she shook her head. 'I swim in private, Mr. Fennel.'

'Aw, come on! You don't imagine I've never seen a naked woman before, and I bet you've seen a naked man.' He grinned fixedly, his face flushed with desire for her. 'You don't have to be coy with me. Strip off, or I'll have to help you.'

Her cool, unafraid gaze disconcerted him.

'You swim . . . I'm going back.'

As she turned away, he caught hold of her wrist.

'You're staying here,' he said, his voice low, and unsteady, 'and you're stripping off. You want some loving, baby, and I'm the guy to give it to you.'

'Take your hand off me,' she said quietly.

'Come on, baby, don't act coy . . . a little loving and then a swim.'

She moved towards him, and for a brief moment, he thought she was going to submit to him. Grinning he released his grip to encircle her waist. Her hand gripped his wrist and an excru-ciating pain shot up his arm, forcing him to cry out. Her foot slapped against his chest as she fell flat on her back. Fennel felt himself shooting into the air and then he splashed into the pool. The cool water closed over him, and when he bobbed to the sur-face and had dashed the water out of his eyes, he found her standing on the bank, looking down at him. Choking with rage, his arm aching, he glared murderously at her, seeing she was holding a large chunk of rock in her hands.

'Stay where you are unless you want your skull cracked,' she said.

Her stillness and her cold eyes warned him she wasn't bluffing.

'You bitch!' he snarled. 'I'll fix you for this!'

'You don't frighten me, you fat animal,' she said scornfully. 'From now on, you leave me alone. If you ever try to touch me again, I'll break your arm. If you weren't so important to this operation, I would have done it just now. Remember that! Now have a swim and cool off, you revolting ape.' She tossed the rock into the water just in front of him, and by the time he had cleared his eyes, she had gone.

Kahlenberg was signing a batch of letters when his office door opened silently and Kemosa came in. He waited patiently in the doorway until Kahlenberg had finished and when Kahlenberg looked up inquiringly he shuffled forward. He put a small glass bottle on the blotter.

'There it is, master.'

Kahlenberg regarded the bottle.

'What is it?'

'The poison you ordered, master.'

'I know that . . . what is the poison?'

Kemosa looked blank.

'That I don't know, master.'

Kahlenberg made an impatient movement.

'Did you tell the witch doctor exactly what I wanted?'

'Yes, master.'

'A poison that would kill a man in twelve hours?'

'Yes, master.'

'Is he to be trusted?'

'Yes, master.'

'What did you pay him?'

'Twenty goats.'

'Did you tell him if the poison doesn't work, he will lose all his goats and I will burn his hut and turn him off my estate?'

'I told him that if the poison doesn't work, two men would come in the night and throw him in the crocodile pool.'

'Does he believe that?'

'Yes, master.'

Kahlenberg nodded, satisfied.

'Go to the medical chest, Kemosa, and bring me a syringe and a pair of rubber gloves.'

When Kemosa had left, Kahlenberg sat back, looking at the small bottle. His mind went back four hundred years. Caesar Borgia might also have contemplated a similar phial of poison, planning the end of an enemy, feeling the same pleasure that Kahlenberg was experiencing.

He was still sitting motionless when Kemosa returned with the syringe and gloves.

'Thank you,' and Kahlenberg waved him away.

When the door had closed, he opened a drawer and took out the glass box containing the ring. He took out the ring and put it on the fourth finger of his right hand. He studied the flashing diamonds thoughtfully, then he turned the ring so the diamonds were worn inside. The plain silver band now showing looked very innocent. He took off the ring and laid it on the blotter. Then he put on the surgical gloves. Screwing the watchmaker's glass into his eye, he slid open the trap in the ring. Then laying the ring down again, he uncorked the bottle and drew some of the colourless liquid into the syringe. Very carefully he inserted the needle of the syringe into the reservoir of the ring and equally carefully pressed the plunger. When, through the watchmaker's glass, he saw the liquid was level with the top of the reservoir, he withdrew the needle and slid the diamond trap into place. Laying down the syringe, he wiped the ring on his handkerchief, taking time over the operation. Still without removing his gloves, he began shaking the ring sharply over the blotter, looking for any signs of a leak in the reservoir. Finally satisfied, he put the ring in a drawer, put his handkerchief in an envelope and sent for Kemosa again. When the old man came in, he told him to destroy the syringe, the poison, the gloves and the handkerchief.

'Make certain they are all destroyed,' he said. 'You understand? Be very careful not to touch the needle of the syringe.'

'Yes, master.'

When he had gone, Kahlenberg took out the ring and regarded it. Was this now a lethal weapon? he asked himself. The witch doctor must be over eighty years of age. Had he lost his cunning? Could he be trusted? If the poison were lethal, could the tiny hollow needle, hidden in the cluster of diamonds, have become blocked with dust? If it had he would be wasting his time, and this was something Kahlenberg never tolerated. He had to know for certain. He sat thinking, then making up his mind, he put the ring on the fourth finger of his right hand and turned the ring the wrong way round. He propelled himself into the garden, followed by Hindenburg.

It took him a little time to find Zwide, a Bantu about whom

Kemosa had often complained, saying this man was not only incurably lazy but also ill-treated his wife. He was due to be dismissed at the end of the month, and to Kahlenberg's callous thinking no loss to anyone.

He found him squatting in the shade, half asleep. When he saw Kahlenberg, he rose hurriedly to his feet, grabbed up a hoe and began feverishly weeding a nearby rose bed.

Kahlenberg stopped his chair beside him. Hindenburg sat, his eyes watchful.

'I hear you are leaving at the end of the month, Zwide,' Kahlenberg said quietly.

The man nodded dumbly, stiff with fear.

Kahlenberg stretched out the ringed hand.

'I wish you good fortune. Shake my hand.'

Zwide hesitated, his eyes rolling with embarrassment, then reluctantly stretched out his hand. Kahlenberg caught the dirty pink palmed hand in a hard, firm grip, his eyes intent on the man's face. He saw him give a little start. Then Kahlenberg released the hand and set the chair in motion. When he had gone a few metres, he looked back.

Zwide was staring with a bewildered expression at his hand and as Kahlenberg watched, Zwide raised a finger to his mouth and licked it.

Kahlenberg went on his way. At least the needle had scratched, he thought. In twelve hours time he would know if the ring was lethal.

As Gaye reached the clearing, she heard the engine of the helicopter start up. She came to a standstill watching the propellers churning. She could see Garry at the controls.

She cried, 'Hey! Wait for me!'

But he didn't hear her. The machine took off, climbing steeply and then went out of sight behind the trees.

Ken and Themba had got the tent up. They had been also watching the take-off. Now they continued to unload the Land Rover. She joined them.

'Why didn't he wait for me?' she asked. 'That was mean!'

Ken grinned.

'You ask him when he comes back. Where's our lovely boy friend?'

'Having a swim.'

There was a note in her voice that made him look sharply at her.

'Trouble?'

'The usual, but I settled it.'

'You're quite a girl.' His look of admiration pleased her.

'Be careful of him . . . he's vicious.'

'Themba and I can take care of him.' He dragged out the four sleeping bags. 'I'm putting yours between Garry's and mine. Themba sleeps next to me . . . then Fennel.'

She nodded.

'It's only for one night, isn't it?'

'Yes . . . for him and me, but two nights for Garry and you.' He looked up at the clouds moving across the sky. 'The sooner we get off the better. If it rains the road will be a real mess. You'll be all right on your own with Garry . . . he's a good guy.'

'I know.'

He took the sleeping bags into the tent and laid them out. Themba was building a fire some little way from the tent. Ken collected the .22 rifle and pocketed some ammunition.

'I'm going after guinea-fowl. Want to come?'

'Of course.'

They set off together into the bush.

Fennel came out of the trees, moving slowly. His arm still ached. He looked around, then seeing only Themba busy with the fire, he went to the Land Rover, got out his rucksack and went into the tent. He changed out of his wet shorts and put on a dry pair. He came out into the dying sunshine and sat on one of the wooden cases. His mind was smouldering. Well, he would fix her, he told himself as he lit a cigarette. There was time. Get the operation over. On the way back, he'd teach her.

He was still sitting there, brooding, when the helicopter came in to land. After a while Garry came over.

'A beauty,' he said enthusiastically. 'Goes like a bird.'

Fennel looked up and grunted.

'Where are the others?'

Fennel shrugged.

'I wouldn't know.'

'How about a beer?'

'Yeah.'

Garry opened the carton. Themba came over with glasses and a thermos of ice. As Garry was opening the bottles, Gaye and

Ken came out of the bush. Ken had four guinea-fowl hanging from a string to his belt.

'Why didn't you wait for me?' Gaye demanded.

Garry shook his head.

'Trial flight. First time I've handled her. Cockeyed for both of us to get killed.'

Gaye's eyes opened wide. She took the beer Themba offered her with a smile. Ken drank from the bottle, sighed, then handed the birds to Themba who took them away.

'We'll eat well tonight,' Ken said and squatted down on the grass. 'Let's talk business, Lew. We two and Themba leave at first light ... around 04.00 hrs. We'll take the rifle and the shotgun, our sleeping bags, rucksacks and food.' He looked over at Garry. 'You any good with a .22?'

Garry grimaced.

'Never tried.'

'I am,' Gaye said. 'I'll get you a guinea-fowl, Garry.'

'That's fine.'

Fennel glanced up, looked at Gaye, then at Garry, then looked away.

'Okay ... anyway, you have only one more day here. The day after tomorrow you take off for Kahlenberg's place.' Ken took a pencil from his pocket and drew a rough circle in the sand. 'I've been talking to Themba. He's been up to Kahlenberg's estate for the past two days.' He glanced over at Lew who was lighting a cigarette. 'You listening, Lew?'

'You think I'm goddamn deaf?'

'This circle represents Kahlenberg's estate. Themba tells me it is guarded by a lot of Zulus south, west and east, but not on the north side. The road into the estate on the north side is reckoned impassable, but Themba has been over it. He says there's one really tricky bit, but if we can't get over it, we can walk. It's our only safe way in.'

'How far do we walk if we can't drive?' Fennel asked, leaning forward as Ken marked a spot on the north side of the circle.

'Twenty kilometres as near as damn it.'

Fennel thought of his heavy tool bag.

'But there's a chance we can get through in the truck?'

'Themba thinks so, so long as it doesn't rain too hard. If it really rains then we are in trouble.'

'Well, some people have all the luck,' Fennel said, looking over at Garry, but Garry wasn't to be drawn. He got up and walked over to watch Themba cooking the birds. He wished he could speak Afrikaans. There was something about the big Bantu's face that appealed to him. As if reading his thoughts, Themba looked up and grinned cheerfully and then continued to turn the spit.

Gaye joined Garry.

'Hmmmm, smells good . . . I'm starving.'

Themba raised a finger and crossed it with a finger of his left hand.

'That means you have to wait half an hour,' Garry said. 'Come over to the chopper. I'll tell you about it.'

They walked over to the helicopter.

Fennel watched them, his eyes glittering. Ken had no desire to talk to him. He went over and joined Themba. They spoke together in Afrikaans.

'Looks like rain soon?' Ken said, squatting beside the Bantu.

'Could come tonight.'

Ken grimaced.

'Well, we've got the winch. If that doesn't pull us out, nothing will.'

'Yes.'

They talked on. Half an hour later, the birds were cooked. It was dark now and the air heavy and close. They all sat around the fire, eating with their fingers. Without Fennel, the party could have been gay, but his dour expression and his silence killed any light-hearted atmosphere.

When they had finished and Themba had cleared up, Ken said, 'I'm turning in. We have to be up early tomorrow.'

'Yes . . . I'm dying to sleep.' Gaye got to her feet.

'Give you five minutes to get into your bag,' Ken said, 'then I'm coming in.'

Gaye disappeared into the tent.

'I guess I'll join you,' Garry said, stretching. 'That was some meal.' He looked at Fennel. 'You turning in?'

'Is the smoke sleeping in there?'

'If you mean is Themba sleeping in there . . . he is.'

Fennel spat in the fire.

'I don't dig breathing the same air as a black man.'

'Okay . . . take your sleeping bag out then.'

Fennel got swiftly to his feet and advanced on Ken, his fists clenched. He was much more powerfully built than Ken who wouldn't have stood a chance against him. Garry stepped between them, facing Fennel.

'I'm getting fed up with you,' he said evenly. 'If you're aching to hit someone, hit me.'

Fennel eyed him, hesitated, then backed away.

'Go to hell,' he growled and sat down. He sat by the dying fire long after the others were sleeping, then finally realizing he must get some sleep, he entered the tent and crawled into his sleeping bag.

Towards 02.00 hrs. the sound of rain drumming on the roof of the tent woke them all.

Above the sound of the rain came the choked roar of a lion.

Chapter Six

Fennel came awake as someone turned on a powerful flashlight. He could see Ken wriggling out of his sleeping bag. Themba held the flashlight and was leaving the tent.

'Time to go?' Fennel asked with a yawn.

'Just about. Themba's getting the breakfast. I'm going down for a swim . . . coming?'

Fennel grunted, slipped on his shoes and shorts and grabbed up a towel. He followed Ken out into the damp half light. It had stopped raining, but the clouds were heavy and swollen.

'Going to be sticky,' Ken said as the two men trotted down to the pool, 'but with the winch, and if we're lucky, we'll make it.'

Reaching the pool, they dived in, swam across, turned and swam back and came out. They towelled themselves vigorously, slipped into their shorts, then trotted back to the camp.

Both Gaye and Garry were up and squatting by the fire watching Themba frying a batch of eggs and bacon.

By the time they had finished breakfast and Themba had cleared up, it was light enough to move.

'Well, let's go,' Ken said. Turning to Garry, he went on, 'Do you think you can get the tent down and fold it?'

'Sure. I'll pack it in the chopper . . . right?'

'If you leave it here, it'll disappear for sure.' Ken looked a Themba. 'All okay?'

Themba nodded.

'Let's synchronize our watches. We'll call you on radio at 11.00 hrs. just to report progress. After that we'll call you every two hours . . . okay?'

They checked their watches, then Garry offered his hand.

'Good luck . . . watch that bastard.'

Fennel was putting his tool kit in the Land Rover. He got in at the back and sat on the bench seat, staring moodily ahead.

'Sweet type, isn't he?' Ken grinned. He turned to Gaye and shook hands. They watched him slide into the driving seat. Themba waved a cheerful hand and got in the front seat beside Ken.

Ken drove into the jungle where it was dark enough for him to put on the headlights. He drove slowly, and Fennel wondered how the hell anyone could know where he was going in this dense jungle. Themba was continually directing Ken. Maybe this blackie wasn't all that of a monkey, Fennel thought. He knew he himself would be helpless on his own, and this thought riled him.

As they progressed, the sun began to come up and Ken switched off the headlights. He was able to increase speed slightly. It was a nagging, bumpy ride and Fennel had to hang on.

Themba suddenly pointed and Ken slowed.

'To your right . . . a rhino!'

Fennel swivelled his head.

Standing not more than twenty metres away was a huge rhinoceros. The ungainly animal slowly turned its head to stare at them. Fennel eyed the big horn and he reached for the Springfield, aware his heart was beginning to thump.

'They're dangerous, aren't they?' he asked, his voice low.

'That's the white rhino. He's docile,' Ken told him. 'It's the black one you have to watch out for.'

He drove on, increasing speed. At this hour the bush seemed alive with game. Herds of impala scattered at the approach of the Land Rover. Two warthogs went crashing into the shrubs, their tails up like periscopes. Black bellied storks watched them from the tree tops. It was as they were nearing the edge of the bush that Themba pointed, and Ken said, 'Lions!'

Lying by the side of the track were two full grown male lions. Fennel calculated they would pass within four metres of them.

'You're not passing those bastards?' he demanded.

'Nothing to worry about,' Ken said cheerfully. 'You leave a lion alone and he'll leave you alone.'

But Fennel wasn't convinced. He picked up the Springfield, his finger curling around the trigger.

They were nearly on the lions now. Both beasts raised their heads and regarded the on-coming Land Rover with sleepy indifference. Fennel felt sweat on his face. As they passed, they were so close he could have touched the lions with the end of the rifle.

'See?' Ken said. 'You don't have to worry about lions, but you wound one and go in after him and you'll have a hell of a lot to worry about.'

Fennel put down the rifle and wiped his sweating face with the back of his hand.

'That was too damn close.'

They came out of the jungle on to a dirt road. Themba indicated that Ken should turn to the right.

'This is the road leading to Kahlenberg's estate ... the whole sixty kilometres of it,' Ken said after he had talked with Themba. He looked at his watch. The time was 08.00 hrs. 'Themba reckons we'll get to the edge of the estate in three hours. We'll radio back to Garry when we get there.'

'Three hours to do sixty kilometres. You nuts?'

'The road's bad. It could take us longer.'

The road was bad, and gradually deteriorated. It was climbing gently all the time. The night's rain had softened the surface and the Land Rover began to slide a little. Ahead of them was a very sharp rise and as Ken increased speed for the run up, the back wheels slid and Ken hurriedly steered into the skid just as it seemed they were about to leave the road.

'Watch what you're doing!' Fennel snarled, startled.

'I can do without a back seat driver,' Ken returned. 'Just shut up, will you?'

The Land Rover crawled up the rise and Ken slammed on his brakes when he saw the dip below was full of water and there was another sharp rise to get out of the dip.

'We're not going through that,' he said and put the truck into reverse, slowly sliding back down the rise. He then drove off the road and on to the tangle of dead branches, shrubs and coarse, rain soaked grass. They hadn't gone more than ten metres when the rear wheels spun and Fennel felt the truck sink.

Ken gave the engine more gas, resulting only in producing a shower of wet, sticky mud that sprinkled them as the wheels spun.

Themba sprang out and went around to the back. Ken engaged gear while Themba pushed, but they only sank deeper.

Ken turned, and as he disengaged gear, he looked straight at Fennel.

'Let's get this straight, Lew. Are you with us or are you just a goddamn passenger?'

Fennel hesitated, then got down from the Land Rover. His bull strength combined with Themba's weight began to tell. There was more splattering of mud, then the tyres got a new purchase and the Land Rover came out of the two holes it had dug. Walking beside it, ready to go into action again, Fennel and Themba, watched warily. Twice the Land Rover skidded but righted itself. They were past the dip now and Ken steered back on the road.

'See what I mean?' he said. 'Twenty minutes wasted.'

Fennel grunted and climbed on board. He was breathing heavily. By now the sun was hot and beat down on them. Ken increased speed and they continued to climb, banging and bumping over the stony road, avoiding the water filled pot-holes where he could, and when he couldn't, banging into them, jolting them all and making Fennel curse.

The road narrowed suddenly and became nothing better than a rough track, strewn with fair-sized boulders. Three times during the next hundred metres, Themba had to jump down and heave the rocks out of the way. They were now crawling at around ten kilometres an hour.

It didn't look to Fennel as if any vehicle had ever come along this narrow track which kept climbing. Branches of trees hung low, causing both men to keep ducking. Themba was walking ahead now as the Land Rover's speed was even more reduced.

'You mean we've got another fifty kilometres of this bitching road to drive on?' Fennel exclaimed as he ducked under another branch.

'That's about it. According to Themba it gets worse as we go on, but at least we are moving.'

That appeared to be a rash thing to have said for almost immediately they struck a soft patch of ground and before Ken could control the skid, they had slid off the narrow track and the off-side wheels slammed down into a gutter.

They stopped.

Themba came running back as Ken got out of the Land Rover. The two men surveyed the position of the wheels and discussed it together while Fennel got down and lit a cigarette. He felt irritatingly useless. To him, they looked stuck for good.

'Only thing to do is to lift her out,' Ken said.

He began to unload the truck, handing the jerrycans of water and gas to Themba. Fennel got the rucksacks, sleeping bags and his heavy tool bag out.

'Back wheels first,' Ken said.

The three men got grips and at Ken's shout, heaved up. Their combined strength lifted the wheels and the next heave got the tail of the truck back on to the road.

'I can pull her out now,' Ken said. 'You two shove against the side in case she slides in again.'

Three minutes later, the Land Rover was once more on the road. They hastily reloaded, then Fennel said, 'I'm having a drink.'

Ken nodded and Themba opened two bottles of beer and a bottle of tonic water for himself.

Fennel looked at Themba.

'You say it's going to get worse?'

'So he says,' Ken broke in. 'No use talking to him, he doesn't understand English.'

Fennel emptied his bottle of beer.

'Looks like we three have picked the crappy end of the stick, doesn't it?' he said.

'That's the way the cookie crumbles.' Ken finished his beer, tossed the bottle into the gutter and climbed under the driving wheel. 'Let's go.'

At least the two incidents seemed to have made Fennel more human, he thought as he engaged gear. He had spoken to Themba and he had shown a spark of comradeship.

They now came to a series of steep hairpin bends. Using the four wheel drive, Ken continued the climb but at not much more than twelve kilometres an hour. The exertion of dragging the wheel around as he came into the bends and then straightening was making him sweat. The bends seemed to go on and on and they climbed higher and higher.

Fennel leaned forward.

'Want me to take a turn? I can handle this crate.'

Ken shook his head.

'Thanks . . . I can cope.' He spoke to Themba in Afrikaans and Themba replied.

Feeling out of it, Fennel demanded, 'What are you talking about?'

'At the top is the bad place. Themba says this is where we could get stuck for good.'

'That's fine! Bad place! What the hell does he call this?'

Ken laughed.

'From what he says, this is like driving down Piccadilly to what we're coming to.'

Then from nowhere grey sluggish clouds crossed the sun, shutting it out and it turned cold. As Ken left the last hairpin bend and started up a long narrow, rocky rise, the rain came down in solid warm sheets.

The three men were soaked to the skin in seconds and Ken, blinded, stopped the Land Rover. They all crouched forward, shielding their faces with their arms while the rain slammed down on their bowed backs. They remained like that for some minutes. Water was in the Land Rover and sloshing around Fennel's shoes, and water lay inches deep on the tarpaulin covering their equipment.

Abruptly as it began, the rain ceased, the clouds moved away and the sun came out. In a very few minutes their clothes began to steam.

'This is one hell of a picnic,' Fennel said. 'My goddamn cigarettes are soaked!'

Ken took a pack from the glove compartment and offered it.

'Take these.'

'I'll take one . . . keep the rest in there. If the bitch is going to start again, we don't want to run short.'

They both lit up and then got back into the truck. Themba had walked on ahead. By now he was at the top of the rise and stood waiting.

As they reached him, he motioned Ken to stop. Both men

looked beyond him at the road ahead. They appeared to be on the top of a mountain and the track abruptly narrowed. One side was a sloping bank of coarse grass and shrubs; the other side was a sheer drop into the valley.

Fennel stood up in the Land Rover and stared at the track. He was never sure of himself when in high places, and the sight of the distant valley far below and the narrowness of the rough track brought him out in a sweat.

'We're bitched!' he said, his voice unsteady. 'We can't hope to get through there!'

Ken turned and looked sharply at him. Seeing his ashen face and how his hands were shaking, he realized this was a man with no head for heights and felt sorry for him.

'Look, Lew, you get out. I think I can get through. It'll be a tight squeeze, but it can be done.'

'Don't be a fool! You'll kill your goddamn self!'

Ken shouted to Themba. 'Can I do it?'

The Bantu stood in the middle of the track and regarded the Land Rover, then he nodded.

'Just,' he said.

'What's he say?' Fennel demanded.

'He thinks it's all right.'

'All right? Hell! You'll go over!'

'You get out.'

Fennel hesitated, then picking up his tool bag, he got down on to the track.

'Wait a minute,' he said, sweat pouring down his face, 'If you're going to kill yourself, I'm going to get all the equipment off first. If she goes over, we'll be stuck without food or drink.'

'Maybe you have something there,' Ken said with a wide grin. He climbed over the back and Themba realizing what they were doing joined them. The three men carefully lifted off the tarpaulin, draining the rain water on to the track, then they hastily unloaded all the equipment.

Fennel glanced at his watch. It was 10.55 hrs.

'We'll have a beer,' he said. 'In five minutes you have to contact Edwards. How much farther have we to go?'

Ken consulted Themba as he opened two beer bottles.

'About twenty kilometres. Then another ten kilometres to the big house,' Themba told him.

Ken translated.

'Rough going?'

Themba said once over this bit the going was good.

They finished the beer and then Ken picked up the two-way radio.

'Ken to Garry . . . are you receiving me?'

Immediately: 'Garry to Ken . . . loud and clear. How goes it?'

Briefly Ken explained the situation.

'Sounds dicey. Look, Ken, why not use the winch? Anchor ahead and wind yourself in. If the truck slips you have a chance to jump.'

'Idea. Roger. Call you back. Out.'

'I bet he feels smug,' Fennel growled. 'Did he say if he's laid that bitch yet?'

'Skip it, Lew,' Ken said impatiently. He talked to Themba who nodded and taking the tarpaulin cover off the winch, he ran the cable out until he was beyond the narrowest part of the track. Ken gave Fennel the drag.

'You any good at splicing? It's got to be secure.'

'I'll fix it.'

Averting his eyes from the drop on his right, Fennel joined Themba, anchor in hand, his tool bag slung over his shoulder. It took him a little over half an hour before he was satisfied. While he worked, Ken sat behind the wheel and smoked. He had steady nerves and was quite cool. He knew there was a risk, but he was also confident that he could get through.

Finally Fennel stood up.

'It's okay.'

He had fixed the drag firmly in a root of a massive tree, growing nearby and using a club hammer, he hammered the drag well home.

He walked back to the Land Rover.

'That won't come out. The cable won't burst. Depends now if the winch gets torn out of its casing.'

'Cheer up,' Ken said, grinning. 'Well, let's try. Will you stay behind me, Lew? If the back begins to slide either correct it or yell to me if you can't. I want Themba ahead to watch the off-side wheels.'

'I'll tell you something,' Fennel said, breathing heavily. 'You've got more bloody guts than I have.'

The two men looked at each other, then Ken turned, set the

engine going, released the handbrake and moved the lever operating the winch forward. The drum began to revolve. He quickly cut the speed of the drum and the Land Rover began to inch forward.

Fennel walked behind, both his hands on the tailboard of the truck, his eyes on Themba who was squatting down, his eyes glued to the front wheels, beckoning Ken on.

The truck covered ten metres before Themba raised his hand sharply to stop.

Ken flicked the winch lever to neutral.

'What's the matter now?' Fennel growled from behind.

Themba had gone to the drag and was looking at it.

'Does that black ape think I would let it pull loose?' Fennel snarled. 'That's in, and it'll stay in!'

'Don't get so worked up,' Ken said, taking out a soiled handkerchief and wiping his face.

Satisfied, Themba went back to the middle of the track.

'Four more metres and you're on the narrow bit,' he called.

Ken set the drum revolving again.

The Land Rover began to crawl forward again. Then the unpredictable happened, three metres before the narrows. The road, sodden by the rain, crumbled under the weight of the truck. Fennel felt the back sliding towards the drop and he threw his weight desperately against the tailboard, trying to steer the truck back, yelling to Ken to jump. He felt himself being dragged to the edge, and shuddering, he let go and rolled on his back towards the grass slope. He was on his feet in an instant, but the Land Rover had gone.

He looked wildly up the road. Themba, on the edge of the drop, was staring down, his big eyes rolling. Cursing, Fennel saw the taut cable was vibrating, and steeling himself, he went to the edge, feeling sick and dizzy, and looked over.

Four metres below, dangling by the cable was the Land Rover. Ken was standing on the back of the seat, his hands gripping the wind shield. Far, far below spread out like an aerial map, was the valley.

Even as he looked, Fennel saw the drum was slowly parting from the casing.

'Get to the drum!' he bawled. 'Ken ... it's coming away! Get the drum!'

Ken balanced himself, stepped over the wind shield and flat-

tened himself up right on the perpendicular bonnet. He caught
hold of one of the steel stanchions supporting the drum, heaved
forward, his hands around the cable of the drum. Even as he got
a grip, the drum parted from the truck and the truck went hurt-
ling down into the void.

Ken swung on the end of the cable. Themba had the cable in
his hands and was trying to haul him in. Shaking from head to
foot, Fennel joined him. Ken swung hard against the side of the
mountain and his feet got a purchase. As the two men hauled, he
began to walk up the slightly sloping side and moments later, he
rolled on to the track.

He sat up and forced a grin.

'Now, we will damn well have to walk,' he said.

As the Land Rover drove into the bush, Gaye sighed with
relief.

'Well, thank goodness, he's out of the way,' she said. 'He was
really beginning to get on my nerves.'

'Mine too.' Garry lit a cigarette. 'Do you want some more
coffee?'

She shook her head.

'When it gets lighter, I'll have a swim. The pool looks marvellous.' She wandered over to the fire and knelt before it.

Garry watched her, thinking how lovely she looked, the flames
of the fire lighting up her face. Then he went into the tent, found
his cordless electric razor and shaved in the light of the flash-
lamp. As he shaved, he thought of the hours ahead of them
before they took off. He was sharply aware that they were alone
together. Firmly, he put the thought out of his mind. Picking up
the towel, he left the tent. The light was brighter now. In another
hour the sun would be up, but he felt in need of cold water and
was too impatient to wait.

'I'll take my swim first,' he called to her. 'Are you all right
alone here?'

'Yes, unless a lion turns up. It'll be cold.'

'That's how I like it.'

She watched him move off into the shadows and she fed the
fire with more sticks collected in a big heap by Themba. She also
thought of the hours ahead. She admitted to herself that Fennel
in his brutish way had stirred a dormant desire in her for a man.
How long, she pondered, had it been since she had had a satisfac-

tory lover? Her mind went back over the number of men who had shared her bed. She could remember only two who had really pleased and satisfied her. The first had been a little like Garry, not so tall and more handsome . . . an American on vacation. She had been in Paris, modelling clothes. On one hot July night, she had been sitting alone at Fouquet's café which had been crowded. He had come up and asked if he could share her table. They had looked at each other, and she knew immediately that she would be sleeping with him within a few hours as he too seemed to know. Again, the second man, also an American and also who had looked a little like Garry, had come out of the dimness of a bar where she had been waiting for friends and had invited her to drink with him. They had left the bar together before her friends arrived. She decided this Garry type of man had sexual attraction for her that sparked with her instantly as two flints struck together will cause a spark.

She had only met these two men once and only knew their Christian names, but the few hours she had spent with them were etched on her mind, and now after that ape Fennel had aroused her after so long, she knew that sometime during the day, Garry would become her lover.

The sun was rising, and already she could feel its warmth. She moved away from the fire and went into the tent to straighten up. By the time she had finished, she could feel the heat of the sun coming through the canvas of the tent and she went out, taking a towel with her.

She saw Garry coming towards her, wearing shorts and shoes, his towel over his shoulder.

She smiled at him.

'Was it good?'

'Marvellous, but cold. It'll be fine now.'

'See you later.' She was aware that he was looking at her as the two Americans had looked at her, then he looked away.

She nodded and ran off, swinging her towel, towards the pool.

She seldom had the opportunity of swimming naked and this she loved to do. She stripped off and dived in. The sun was fully on the pool by now and the chill was off the water. She swam for some time, then turned on her back, closed her eyes and let herself float.

Two grey, black-faced monkeys high up in a tree watched her.

Then as if by agreement, they slid down the tree, moved swiftly to where she had left her shorts, shirt and towel, snatched them up and shinned up the tree again. Having examined the clothes and finding them of no interest, they left them hanging on a high branch and went swinging from tree to tree farther into the forest.

As they went, Gaye opened her eyes and saw them. She watched them, thinking how cute they looked, but she didn't think them cute when, on climbing out of the pool, she found only her shoes on the bank.

Looking up, she caught sight of her towel hanging on a branch. She hesitated, knowing she could never climb up there, then shrugging, she put on her shoes and walked back to the camp. Garry, sitting in the shade of the tent, was examining the aerial map Shalik had given him. He glanced up as she came out of the line of trees and startled, he dropped the map. For a moment, he couldn't believe his eyes, then he got to his feet.

Quite unconcerned, naked as she was born, Gaye came on.

'Monkeys have stolen my clothes . . . the little devils. They are up a tree by the pool. Could you get them for me, Garry?' she called as she was half-way across the plain. She made no attempt to hide her nakedness. Her arms swung loosely at her sides as she moved. She behaved as if she were fully dressed.

'Sure . . .'

He started towards her, then deliberately made a wide half circle so he wouldn't pass close to her and she liked him for that.

They passed and she went into the tent. She was quite sure he hadn't looked back at her. Her heart was beating fast. She went to her rucksack to get her duplicate shirt and shorts. She got them out, looked at them, hesitated, then dropped them to the ground and stretched herself out on top of her sleeping bag. With her legs crossed and her hands covering her breasts, she waited his return.

'It's nearly 11.00 hrs.,' Garry said. 'They will be coming through on the radio.'

She was loath to let him go, but as he moved away from her, she let her arms slide away from his body. She watched him stand up and put on his shorts, then she closed her eyes.

She had been right about him. It had been even better than it had been with the other two Americans, and also, she did know his surname. The tensions that had been building up inside her for the past year had been released by the explosive coupling, and now she felt as if she had had a shot of some hard drug. She didn't wish to be disturbed, but to be allowed to remain still and to do nothing. She drifted off into semi-sleep which was all the more relaxing and pleasant in the heat of the tent.

She was startled awake by Garry coming to the opening of the tent and calling her name sharply.

She half sat up and immediately became fully alert at the sight of his worried expression.

'What is it?'

'Those three are in trouble. Put your things on and come out. It's too damn hot in here.'

There was a hard note in his voice and she could see he was impatient with her lying there like a cat before a fire. She slipped into her clothes and came out to join him in the shade.

'The road collapsed, and they've lost the Land Rover,' Garry told her. 'Ken was nearly killed.'

'Is he hurt?'

'No . . . shaken, but all right, now they'll have to walk and it's a hell of a walk.'

'But they'll get there?'

'They think so. They'll be contacting me again in two hours.'

'And the equipment?'

'That's all right. They unloaded before attempting to get over the worst part of the track.'

'How will they get back?'

'We'll all have to fly out . . . nothing else for it. It'll be a load, but it can be done.'

She relaxed, resting her back against the tree.

'So it really isn't so bad . . . they'll just have to walk.'

'In this heat, it won't be so good.'

'Oh, well . . . get some of that ape's fat off. Do you know how to pluck and draw a bird, Garry?'

'No . . . do you?'

'No. So we won't bother to hunt guinea-fowl. We'll have beans and bacon for lunch.' She got to her feet. 'I'm going to have another swim . . . coming?'

He hesitated. 'Those three are worrying me, Gaye.'

'Then a swim with me will put them out of your mind. There's nothing we can do for them . . . so come on and swim.'

She went into the tent for the towels and then together they walked in the burning sun towards the pool.

Fennel wished now he hadn't drunk so much beer in the past. The rough, stony track, the hot sun and the pace that Ken was setting all reminded him of how out of condition he was. The strap of his tool bag was rubbing his shoulder raw. Sweat streamed down his face and blackened his shirt. He was breathing heavily.

At a guess, he thought, they had covered only six kilometres. Ken had talked of thirty kilometres before they reached Kahlenberg's place. Twenty-four kilometres! Fennel gritted his teeth. He was certain he couldn't do it with this tool kit: it got heavier and heavier with every step he took. Apart from his tool kit, he was also carrying his rucksack.

Before setting off, they had decided to leave the sleeping bags and the shotgun. Ken carried the Springfield and his own rucksack, Themba was carrying a rucksack stuffed with provisions and a five litre jerrycan of water.

Fennel plodded on, dragging one foot after the other. He longed for some shade, but there was none on this narrow track. He badly wanted a drink and thought regretfully of the beer they had left behind them. He had wanted it along with them, but when Ken said it was okay with him if Fennel would carry it, Fennel decided against the idea.

He paused to wipe the sweat out of his eyes and was stung with mortification to see the other two walking and chatting together, well ahead of him.

Ken glanced back and then stopped. Themba continued on for a few steps and then he stopped.

Fennel felt a spurt of rage go through him. He came plodding up to them. One look at his exhausted face told Ken that he was going to be a liability. Themba thought so too, and putting down the jerrycan he said something to Fennel who didn't understand.

'He says he'll carry your tool bag if you'll carry the jerrycan,' Ken translated.

Fennel hesitated, but he knew the bag now was too much for him.

'What makes him think *he* can carry it?' he demanded, lowering the bag thankfully to the ground.

'He wouldn't make the offer if he didn't,' Ken pointed out as Themba hoisted up the bag and slung it on his shoulder.

Fennel hesitated, then said, 'Well, tell him ... thanks. It's a bitch of a thing to carry.' He caught hold of the jerrycan and the three men continued on their way: the other two slowing down to keep pace with Fennel.

The next hour was a hellish up-hill grind for Fennel, but he kept plodding on, breathing heavily, furious with himself to see how easily the other two were taking the ordeal.

'How about a drink?' he gasped, coming to a halt.

But the drink gave him no satisfaction as the water was warm and anyway, Fennel loathed drinking water.

Ken looked at his watch.

'In another ten minutes, we'll call Garry. Then we'll have a rest.'

'That guy must have been born lucky,' Fennel growled, picking up the jerrycan. 'He doesn't know how well off he is.'

They continued on, and at 13.00 hrs., they left the track and sat down in the shade of the jungle. Ken contacted Garry and reported progress.

'We should be in position by 18.00 hrs.,' he said, and added the going was rough.

Garry made sympathetic noises, said he would be standing by at 15.00 hrs. and switched off.

After half an hour's rest, they continued on for another hour, then Ken said it was time to eat. They left the sun soaked track and sat down in the shade of the trees. Themba opened cans of steak pie and baked beans.

'How much farther?' Fennel asked, his mouth full.

Ken consulted Themba.

'About six kilometres and then we'll be in the jungle.'

'Ask him if he wants me to carry the bag again.'

'He's okay ... don't bother about it.'

'Ask him! That bag's goddamn heavy!'

Ken spoke to Themba who grinned and shook his head.

'Black people are used to carrying white men's burdens,' Ken said, keeping his face straight.

Fennel eyed him.

'Okay, I'll take that ... so he's a better man than I am.'

'Skip it or I'll burst into tears.'

Fennel smiled sourly.

'My time's coming. You two may be pretty hot with this jungle and walking crap, but you wait until you see me in action.'

Ken offered his pack of cigarettes and the two men lit up.

'Do you think he's giving it to her?' Fennel asked abruptly. When not on his discomforts, his mind kept returning to Gaye.

'Who's giving what to whom?' Ken asked blandly.

Fennel hesitated, then shrugged. 'Forget it!'

An hour later, they again contacted Garry and again reported progress, then they left the mountain track and entered the jungle. Although it was steamy hot, the relief of constant shade helped them to quicken their pace.

Themba led the way with Ken and Fennel following. A narrow track through the dense undergrowth forced them to walk in single file. Overhead, Vervet monkeys swung from tree to tree, watching them. A big sable buck that was standing in the middle of the track as they rounded a high shrub went crashing away into the jungle, startling Fennel.

They had to keep a watch-out for shrubs with long, sharp thorns, and they all concentrated on the ground ahead of them. None of them suspected that they were being watched. High on a branch of a tree sat a giant Zulu, wearing only a leopard skin. In his right hand, he held a two-way radio. He waited until the three men had passed, then spoke rapidly into the mouthpiece of the radio, his message being picked up by Miah, Kahlenberg's secretary, who had been detailed to keep in touch with the twenty watching Zulus positioned to report the movements of strangers on the estate.

From the moment the three men entered the jungle, they were never out of sight from the watchful eyes of the Zulus, hidden in the undergrowth or concealed in the tree tops.

Miah took down the Zulus' reports in rapid shorthand, passed them to Ho-Du who rapidly transcribed them on a typewriter and then had them sent immediately to Kahlenberg.

Kahlenberg was enjoying this. The drama of the Land Rover had been observed and reported to him, and now he knew these three men were actually on his estate.

He turned to Tak.

'The Bantu is expendable,' he said. 'Give the order that if the occasion presents itself, he is to be got rid of. As he seems to be acting as a guide, it is unlikely the others will be able to find their way out without him.'

Tak picked up a two-way radio and spoke softly into it.

While he was speaking, Ken called a brief rest as they reached a clearing in the jungle. The three men sat down in the shade and all took a drink of water.

Ken talked to Themba for a few minutes. Themba pointed. Ahead of them was a narrow track that led into dense undergrowth.

'That's the track that leads directly to Kahlenberg's place,' Ken explained to Fennel. 'We can't miss it. We'll leave Themba here, and we'll go on. If we come unstuck, I don't want him involved. When we have done the job, we'll pick him up here and he'll guide us out. Okay?'

'You're sure we can find our way without him?'

'We follow the track. It leads directly to the house.'

'Well, okay.' Fennel looked at his watch. 'How long will it take to get to the house?'

'About two hours. We'll go now. We'll get near enough to the house before dark.'

Fennel grunted and got to his feet.

Ken talked again to Themba who grinned, nodding his head.

'We'll take some food with us. I've got a water bottle,' Ken said, turning to Fennel. 'You'll have to carry your kit again.'

'Okay, okay, I'm not a cripple.'

Themba put some canned food into Ken's rucksack.

'We'll leave our other stuff here,' Ken went on, shouldering the rucksack, 'and the rifle.' He shook hands with Themba. Speaking in Afrikaans, he said, 'We'll be back the day after tomorrow night. If we are not back in four days, go home.'

Fennel came up to Themba. He looked slightly embarrassed as he pointed to his bag of tools, then grinning sheepishly, he offered his hand. Themba was delighted and grinning widely, he gripped the offered hand.

As he fell into step beside Ken, Fennel said, 'I was wrong about him . . . he's a good man.'

'We all make mistakes,' Ken looked at Fennel with a sly grin. 'I seemed to have been wrong about you.'

Themba watched them walk into the jungle and disappear. He

set out collecting sticks for the fire he would light at dusk. He liked being on his own and was always at home in the jungle. He was slightly curious why the two white men had gone off on their own, but decided it was no business of his. He was being well paid for acting as a guide, and already Ken had given him enough money to enable him to buy a small car when he returned to Durban where he rented a bungalow in which his wife and son lived. He didn't see much of them as he was constantly on various game reserves in the district, but every other week-end, he would come home ... something he always looked forward to.

He made a neat pile of sticks near the tree where the equipment was stacked, then moved into the jungle to find a few dead branches to give guts to the fire.

Suddenly he paused to listen. Something had moved not far from him. His keen ears had distinctly heard the rustle of leaves. A baboon? he wondered. He stood motionless, looking in the direction of the sound.

Out of a thicket behind him, rose a Zulu, wearing a leopard skin across his broad muscular shoulders. The sun glittered on the broad blade of his assagai. For a brief moment, he balanced the heavy stabbing spear in his huge black hand, then threw it with unerring aim and with tremendous force at Themba's unprotected back.

High in the evening sky, six vultures began to circle patiently.

Chapter Seven

'There it is on your right,' Garry said suddenly.

Gaye peered through the helicopter's window. They were flying over dense jungle, and as Garry banked, the jungle abruptly terminated and she could see acres of rich green lawns, green cement paths and vast beds of flowers that would have done credit to a botanical garden. Beyond the lawns she saw the one storey house which was built in a slight curve, and from this height, seemed to her, to be at least seventy metres long. Behind the house, some two hundred metres away were numerous small bungalows with thatched roofs and white painted walls in which she supposed the staff lived.

'It's enormous!' she exclaimed. 'What an extraordinary shape! Imagine walking from one end to the other several times a day.'

'Perhaps they use skates,' Garry said. 'It's certainly big.' He circled the house again. They could see a swimming-pool, terraces, sun umbrellas and lounging chairs. 'We'd better get down. Are you nervous?'

She shook her head, smiling.

'Not a bit ... excited. I wonder if we'll get in.'

'You've got to get us in,' Garry said.

He spotted the airfield and a hangar. As he came lower, he saw three Zulus in white drill, staring up at the helicopter.

He landed not far from them and as he slid back the door, he saw a jeep coming along the road from the house, driven by a Zulu with a white man in a grey city-suit sitting at his side.

'Here comes the welcoming committee,' he said and dropped to the ground.

Gaye handed him down the Rolleiflex camera and her camera bag, and then joined him on the runway as the jeep pulled up.

Tak got out of the jeep and came towards them. Leaving Garry, Gaye advanced to meet him.

'I am Gaye Desmond of Animal World magazine,' she said and held out her hand.

Tak regarded her, thinking she was even more lovely than her photograph. He took her hand briefly and gave her a little bow.

'I apologize for landing like this,' Gaye went on. There was something about this tall man that she instantly distrusted and disliked. 'I'm on my way to Wannock Game Reserve, and I saw this lovely house and just couldn't resist calling. If I shouldn't have, please tell me, and I will leave at once.'

'Not at all, Miss Desmond,' Tak said silkily. 'We seldom have such a beautiful visitor. Now you are here, I hope you will stay to lunch.'

'How nice of you! We would love to, Mr. ...' She looked inquiringly at him.

'Guilio Tak.'

She turned to Garry who joined them.

'Mr. Tak, this is Garry Edwards, my pilot.'

Again Tak bowed.

'Mr. Tak has kindly invited us to lunch.'

Garry shook hands with Tak. He too didn't like the look of him.

Gaye went on, 'The house is marvellous and so isolated! I couldn't believe my eyes when I saw it. Have you had it long, Mr. Tak?'

'This is not my residence, Miss Desmond. It belongs to Mr. Max Kahlenberg.'

Gaye stared at him, her eyes widening.

'You mean the millionaire? *The* Mr. Max Kahlenberg?'

The expression in his black eyes was slightly sardonic as Tak said, 'That is correct.'

'But I have heard he is a recluse!' Gaye said. Watching her, Garry thought she was putting over the act well. 'We'd better go. We mustn't disturb him.'

'You won't do that. Mr. Kahlenberg is not a recluse. I am sure he will be pleased to meet you.'

'Would it be possible to photograph the house. I also freelance for *Life*. It would be a marvellous scoop for me.'

'That you must ask Mr. Kahlenberg. But don't let us stand here in the sun.' Tak moved to the jeep. 'I will take you to the house.'

Gaye and Garry got in the back seat and Tak beside the driver. The Zulu turned the jeep and sped back down the road.

A few minutes later, Gaye and Garry were being ushered into a huge lounge which led through wide french windows to a flower ladened terrace with a big swimming-pool. The luxury of the room stunned Garry who had never seen anything to compare with it and even impressed Gaye who had been in many luxurious homes in her time.

'If you would wait here, I will tell Mr. Kahlenberg of your arrival.'

A Zulu in white drill came in silently.

'Have a drink please while you are waiting,' Tak continued and then went away.

The Zulu went behind the bar and stood waiting.

They asked for two gin and tonics and then moved out on to the terrace.

'I don't like the look of that guy,' Garry said in a low whisper. 'There's something about him . . .'

'Yes. He gives me the creeps. He looks as if he sleeps in a coffin.'

'Don't you think we got in very easily?' Garry went on, pulling up a basket chair for Gaye and then sitting down himself.

'It's my charm.' Gaye smiled. 'I'm irresistible to spooks. The chances are we will be thrown out as soon as Mr. K. hears we have arrived. Tak must be his major-domo or secretary I suppose.'

The Zulu brought the drinks with two plates of delicious looking canapés and silently withdrew.

'What a gorgeous way to live!' Gaye sighed. 'I adore this place. Wouldn't you love to own it?'

Garry sipped his drink, then shook his head.

'Not for me. I like something a bit more rugged. This is too lush.'

'Oh, no!' She helped herself to a cracker covered with caviar. 'I think it is marvellous.'

They had eaten most of the canapés and had finished their drinks before Tak appeared again.

'Mr. Kahlenberg is happy to have you here, Miss Desmond,' he said. 'Unfortunately, he is tied up with a series of long distance calls and other business and won't be free to meet you until tonight. Is it possible for you to stay?'

'You mean . . . stay the night?' Gaye asked, looking up at the pale face.

'Certainly. That is what Mr. Kahlenberg suggests.'

'But I have no clothes with me.'

'That is no problem. We have a number of women secretaries here. One of them will gladly lend you something.'

'How nice! Did you ask him if I could take photographs?'

Tak shook his head.

'I thought it would come better if the request came from you, Miss Desmond.'

'Well, then we will stay the night. It is very kind of Mr. Kahlenberg.'

'It will be his pleasure.' Tak glanced at his watch. 'Lunch will be served in an hour. Perhaps you would care to change?'

As they got to their feet, Tak turned to Garry.

'You too, of course, have no clothes with you, Mr. Edwards?'

'Only what I've got on.'

'That can be arranged.' Tak turned as Miah came out on to the terrace. 'This is Miss Das. She will take care of you both. If you will excuse me now,' and with a stiff little bow, Tak left them.

Miah came forward.

'Please follow me.'

She led them across the lounge into a wide corridor that stretched away into the far distance. What looked like an electric golf cart stood nearby and she slid under the driving wheel while the other two took the rear seats.

'This corridor is so long,' she said, turning to smile at them, 'we have to use this to save our legs.'

'I was wondering how you managed,' Gaye returned. 'When I saw the house from the air, I thought of the tremendous amount of walking it must make.'

Silently the trolley took them quickly past many closed doors until they reached the far end.

'This is the guest wing,' Miah said, stopping the car. She walked to a door and opened it. 'Please come in.'

They entered a long narrow luxuriously furnished room which led on to a small terrace, also with a swimming-pool and a bar.

'You will find everything you want here,' Miah said. 'Your lunch will be served on the terrace at 13.00 hrs. This is your bedroom, Miss Desmond.' She crossed the room and opened a door. 'I will send a maid to help you dress. I thought it would be the easiest thing for you to wear one of my saris. Would that be all right?'

'It would be perfect.' Gaye stood in the doorway looking into the bedroom. It was a delightful room, decorated in pale-blue with a king's size bed, closets, a big dressing-table on which stood a variety of face creams, lotions, perfumes and a make-up kit in a flat, silver box. Moving around the room, Gaye saw on the opposite wall, facing the bed a huge mirror which made the room seem to be twice its size. The bathroom was equipped with every luxury, including a sun lamp, a cabinet equipped with nozzles from which hot air could be released thus saving the fatigue of drying oneself on a towel, and a vibro-massage machine.

While Gaye was exclaiming over the room, Garry was moving

around the sitting-room, making a careful examination of the doors and windows.

Miah came to show him his bedroom and bathroom, both of them as luxurious as Gaye's.

A tall Zulu maid came in carrying the sari. Gaye said she didn't need her help and could manage on her own. A Zulu manservant brought Garry a pair of white slacks, heelless slippers and a white shirt.

'Mr. Kahlenberg is quite informal,' Miah said. 'Dinner tonight will be on the main terrace. Please make yourselves at home. If you wish to swim, there are swim suits in the changing-room. Do explore the garden. If there is anything you wish for, please use the telephone.' With a nod of her head and a smile, she left the room.

Gaye and Garry looked at each other and Garry whistled.

'Talk about living it up . . .'

There came a tap on the door and a Zulu came in with their rucksacks. These he set on the floor and withdrew.

Garry went quickly to his rucksack and satisfied himself the two-way radio hadn't been removed. He looked at Gaye.

'I wonder if they spotted this?'

'It doesn't matter if they did, does it?' Gaye's mind was occupied with the luxury surrounding her. Her eyes shining, she went on, 'Isn't it really marvellous! I'm taking a bath. See you later.' Picking up her rucksack, she went into her bedroom and shut the door.

She quickly undressed. Naked, she stood for a moment admiring herself in the big mirror, then she went into the bathroom and turned on the bath taps. Again while waiting for the bath to fill, she regarded herself in the mirror, striking poses and laughing happily to herself.

What she didn't realize was that both the big mirrors were two-way: anyone behind the mirrors could see her as if the mirrors were plain glass, whereas from the front she imagined the mirrors were genuine and not trick ones.

His affairs forgotten, his desk neglected, Kahlenberg sat in his wheelchair in a narrow passage which was air conditioned and took his fill of Gaye's naked beauty.

From the edge of the jungle, Fennel watched the helicopter land. He and Ken had found a vantage point on a big balancing rock, formed by soil erosion, surrounded by trees and bushes, yet giving them an excellent view of Kahlenberg's house, garden and airfield far below them.

Fennel had powerful field glasses to his eyes. He saw Tak arrive in the jeep and Gaye meet him. He watched Gaye and Garry get into the jeep and drive to the house. He saw them enter and the front door close.

'Good for them! They're in!' he said, lowering the glasses.

'That was pretty easy, wasn't it?' Ken asked, puzzled. 'From what I hear of Kahlenberg, he doesn't welcome strangers.'

'Shalik said he was a sucker for a glamour puss. Looks like Shalik knew what he was talking about.'

'Yes ... but I didn't think it would be that easy.' Ken picked up the two-way radio. 'I'll keep this switched on. Garry may be coming through any time now.'

Fennel lit a cigarette and stretched out on the rock. He was feeling tired after the long walk, carrying his tool bag. He dozed while Ken kept watch. After some little time, Fennel sat up, lit a cigarette, yawned, then asked, 'When you've got the money, what are you going to do with it?'

'A pal of mine in Jo'burg is starting a travel agency,' Ken told him. 'He needs more capital. I'm going into partnership with him.'

'Travel agency? Is that so hot?'

'It's good. We plan a de luxe service. Personally conducted tours around the game reserves. That's where I'll score. There's a lot of money in it. The Americans are heavy spenders if you give them real personal service. I've been dealing with them for some years. I know what they want, and I plan to give it to them.'

Fennel grunted.

'Sounds like hard work to me. I don't believe in work. Only suckers work.'

'So what are you going to do with your share?'

'Spend it ... that's what money is for. I've got no time for the punks who save their money. What happens? They kick off and some other punk gets it.'

'Maybe that's what they want.'

'To hell with that! There's always money around. When I've spent what I get from Shalik, I'll do another little job. I've got plenty of contacts. They know I'm good so I'm never short of a job.'

Ken held up his hand, cutting him short. He had heard a crackle on the two-way radio and he put the set to his ear.

'Ken ... hi, Garry ... hearing you loud and clear ... over.' He listened for some moments while Fennel watched him intently. 'Roger. Good luck. Out,' and he switched off.

'Well?'

'They're staying the night,' Ken told him. 'Kahlenberg seems pleased they dropped in. I must say that surprises me. Anyway, they are meeting him at 21.00 hrs. Garry says he'll call back at 23.00 hrs., and for us to stand by.'

Fennel grunted. He looked at his watch. It was just after midday.

'You mean we stay on this goddamn rock for twelve hours?'

'I guess so. We don't want to walk into any of the guards. I reckon it is safe up here. Let's eat.' He brought out the inevitable can of beans.

'Goddamn it! Isn't there anything else to eat except beans?'

'Steak pie ... want that?'

'That's better than beans.' Fennel brooded as Ken searched in the rucksack for the can. 'I bet those two are doing themselves well.' His mind dwelt on Gaye and a vicious spurt of rage ran through him. Get this job over, he told himself, and then you fix her and you fix her good.

'What's bitten you?' Ken asked, seeing the savage expression on Fennel's face.

'Nothing ... how much longer are you going to take to open that can?'

'I wish I knew we weren't going to be disturbed,' Garry said.

Gaye and he were sitting on the terrace after an excellent lunch served by two Zulu waiters.

Gaye was stretched out on a reclining chair, a cigarette between her fingers. Garry thought she looked lovely in the red and gold sari. It was the type of costume that suited her, and which he admired.

'Why?' Gaye asked, looking at him.

'Obvious reasons,' Garry returned with a grin. 'I would take you into the bedroom.'

She laughed.

'Then I too wish we knew we weren't going to be disturbed.'

'Could be embarrassing if Mr. Tak arrived on the scene.'

'It could. So instead, we had better do some work.' She sat up, crushing out her cigarette. 'Have you thought about how Fennel is to get in?'

'Through here.' Garry waved his hand to the big lounge. 'With us here, he has only to walk in.'

'Would it be as easy as that?'

'I think so. There could be guards patrolling the house at night. I don't see any of them around now.'

'Perhaps Kahlenberg is so sure no one could get through the jungle, the house isn't guarded.'

'Want to take a look at the garden?'

'Not now. It will be terribly hot out there.'

'Then you take a nap . . . I'm going.' Garry got to his feet.

'You have more energy than I have. You'll be roasted.'

'See you,' and with a wave of his hand, Garry wandered off down the green cement path.

She watched him go, then she closed her eyes and thought about him. When the job was done, they would all separate. She wondered what he would do. She would have liked to have had a long week-end with him in Paris, and then say good-bye. She was twenty-six years of age, and she was sure Shalik would continue to make use of her for at least five more years before he began to look around for a younger woman. She had no illusions about Shalik. In those five years she would have made and saved enough money to give her complete independence and that was what she wanted more than anything else. To be financially free to live well, to travel and possibly get married.

She considered the possibility of marrying Garry, but decided it wouldn't work out. Although he attracted her physically, she knew she wasn't in love with him and also he hadn't her need for gracious living. Luxury was essential to her whereas it wasn't to him. No . . . he was a good bed companion, but nothing else. If she were to marry, she must find a man who was wealthy, intelligent, cultured and luxury loving. She knew this was a pipe dream for she had met many men in her life, had many proposals of marriage, but there was always some snag, or was it that she valued her freedom too much?

Anyway, pipe dreams were pleasant when lying in a comfortable chair in the shade, surrounded by luxury.

She dozed off, and it was more than an hour later that Garry, returning, awakened her.

'Want a drink, lazybones?' he asked, moving to the bar.

She nodded, stretched and sat up.

'Find anything interesting?'

'Yes and no. There's no access to the far end of the house.' Garry brought over two Tom Collins and sat down. 'The path leading to it is guarded by a Zulu who looks as if he's stepped right out of a movie. He was wearing a leopard skin, ostrich plumes and carried a shield and an assagai. He turned me back without trying to be polite.'

'Kahlenberg's quarters, I suppose.'

'Yes. Another thing: there's a big pool full of enormous croco-diles at the far end of the garden and sitting on surrounding trees are about ten well fed looking vultures. That corner of the garden gave me the creeps.'

Gaye laughed.

'But why?'

'Just struck me it would be a marvellous place to dispose of a body.'

She looked at him and seeing he was serious, she asked, 'Why should Kahlenberg want to dispose of a body?'

Garry sipped his drink, then cradling the glass in his hand, shaking it slightly so the ice cubes tinkled, he shrugged.

'The atmosphere of the place made me think of it, but I'm uneasy about all this, Gaye. I think we were invited in too easily. I don't like the look of Tak. Once or twice while you were talking to him, I got the idea he was laughing at you. Particularly when you asked if this place was his. It struck me he knew you knew it belonged to Kahlenberg.'

'Do you think he suspects us?'

'I think he could.'

'You don't think he guesses we are after the ring?'

'I don't know, but I'm pretty sure he thinks we are phonies.'

'So what do we do?'

As if in answer to this question, Garry saw Tak coming along the path towards them.

'Here he is now,' he said, getting to his feet.

'Please don't let me disturb you,' Tak said, approaching. There was a thin smile on his lips and his glittering eyes moved from Garry to Gaye. 'Did you enjoy your lunch?'

'It was wonderful, thank you.' Gaye gave him her most charm-ing smile. 'It really is lovely here.'

121

'Yes ... it is very pleasant.' He paused, then went on, 'Miss Desmond, would you be interested to see Mr. Kahlenberg's museum?'

Although her heart skipped a beat, Gaye kept her face mildly interested.

'Has Mr. Kahlenberg a museum?'

'Mr. Kahlenberg is one of the most famous collectors in the world.'

'I knew that, but I didn't know he had a museum. I thought ...'

'He has a museum, and he wondered if it would interest you to see it.'

'Very much. I would love to see it.'

'And you, Mr. Edwards?'

'Sure ... thanks.' Garry kept his expression dead-pan, but like Gaye, he had been startled.

Gaye got to her feet. 'Is it far from here?'

Again Garry caught a jeering expression come into the dark eyes. It came and went so quickly unless he had been watching closely he wouldn't have seen it.

'You are standing on it,' Tak said.

'You mean it is underground?'

'That is correct.'

'May I bring my camera, Mr. Tak?'

He shook his head.

'I regret not.' He turned. 'Will you follow me, please?'

He entered the lounge and walked into the corridor.

Gaye and Garry exchanged swift glances as they followed him. They all got into the electric trolley and Tak drove down the long corridor, past the big lobby and front door of the house and on down the corridor.

'Here is where Mr. Kahlenberg has his quarters,' he explained as they drove past several doors. He stopped the trolley by what appeared to be a blank wall and got out. Watching him closely, Garry saw him put his fingers under the ledge of one of the big windows. The wall he was facing slid back to reveal double doors. As he approached these doors, they slid open.

'Mr. Kahlenberg is a cripple,' Tak explained, regarding Gaye. 'All doors in his quarters are electronically controlled. This is the elevator that takes us down to the museum.'

The three entered the green satin lined cage. There were four different coloured buttons on the control panel. Garry watched Tak press the green button and the elevator descended smoothly, and silently. While it descended Tak pressed the red button, paused, then pressed the yellow button.

'What are all those buttons for, Mr. Tak?' Gaye asked innocently.

'The green button controls the elevator. The yellow button turns on the lights in the museum and the red button turns off the alarm,' Tak told her.

'Thank you . . . you're marvellously well equipped.'

The doors slid back and they entered a cool, vaulted chamber.

'Would you wait here for a moment?' Tak said and he crossed to a grey painted door. He spent a minute or so at the door, his hands busy, his body concealing what he was doing.

Again Garry looked at Gaye, lifted his eyebrows, then looked away as Tak turned.

'The museum contains many priceless treasures,' he said. 'We have taken every precaution against theft. This door that leads into the museum is armour plated and specially treated to make it impossible to cut into. The walls either side are five feet thick. The lock to the door is controlled by a time switch which is set every night at 22.00 hrs. and no one can open the door until 10.00 hrs. the following day. Please come in.'

They followed him into a vast domed ceiling room, lit by diffused lighting. On the walls hung many pictures. Gaye recognized a Rembrandt, several Picassos and a number of Renaissance masterpieces which she was sure she had seen in the Uffizi, the Vatican museum and the Louvre.

'These aren't the originals, Mr. Tak?' she asked.

'Of course they are the originals.' Tak frowned as if annoyed by such a question. 'I told you Mr. Kahlenberg has the finest private museum in the world. The inner room will amuse you more I think.' He led the way through the picture gallery and entered another vast room.

In the middle of the room stood a four metre high Buddha in shining gold.

'This is an interesting piece,' Tak went on. 'It comes from Bangkok. During the last war, the Japanese, knowing it was in the city, searched for it, but the priests were too clever for them. They moved it to a lesser temple and covered it with dirty cement. Although the Japanese visited this temple they failed to recognize what they were looking for.'

'You mean this is solid gold?' Garry said, gaping at the glittering figure.

'Yes, it is solid gold.'

He led them around the room, pausing to explain various objets d'art. Garry had no knowledge of art treasures, but even he was impressed by what he saw.

'But surely that is one of the panels of Ghiberti's Gates to Paradise,' Gaye said, pausing before a beautifully carved panel on the wall. 'What a wonderful copy!'

'The copy is in Florence, Miss Desmond. This is the original,' Tak said, an acid note in his voice. 'And this statue of David by Bernini is also the original. The copy is in the Bargello in Florence.'

Gaye was so startled by the effrontery of this remark, that she turned away. It was then she caught sight of the Caesar Borgia ring in a small glass box on a pedestal in the lighted alcove. 'And what is this?' she asked, moving to the glass box and peering at the ring.

'The Caesar Borgia ring,' Tak said. 'It was made by an unknown goldsmith at Borgia's request. It is a poison ring and so the story goes, the goldsmith was its first victim. To test its efficiency and to stop the man from talking, Borgia gave him his fatal handshake while wearing the ring. There is a needle hidden in the cluster of diamonds and this scratched the victim's hand while he was shaking hands with Borgia. Ingenious, don't you think?'

'Those were cruel, horrible times,' Gaye said with a little grimace. 'Is it dangerous now?'

'Oh no, Miss Desmond. It would have to be recharged with poison before it could be dangerous, and I doubt if the needle is now sharp enough to scratch.'

He led them on, showing them a beautiful alabaster unguent jar which he told them came from the tomb of Tutankhamen. They spent a further half-hour in the museum and then Tak, looking at his watch, suggested they might like a drink before dinner. He led them from the museum, closed the door and Garry watched him spin the dial, scrambling the combination, then they took the elevator up to the corridor. He drove them back to their suite and after accepting their thanks, said a servant would conduct them to the main terrace in an hour and a half and left them.

The time now was 19.30 hrs. and they both went out on to the terrace.

'I want something short and strong,' Gaye said sitting down. 'A vodka martini on the rocks.'

'I'll dig for that too.' Garry began to mix the drink. He filled two cocktail glasses and carried them over to the table and sat down. 'Did you spot the TV snoopers in both rooms?'

'No . . . did you?'

'Yes. Fennel said there were six monitors and therefore six rooms in the museum. Tak only showed us two of the rooms. You know, Gaye I'm liking this less and less. I have an idea we could have walked into a trap.'

Gaye looked startled.

'Surely not! He wouldn't have shown us what he did if he is really suspicious of us.'

'That's what puzzles me. He must realize we have guessed most of those exhibits have been stolen. Then why did he let us see them? Why did he tell us how the elevator works and about the time lock? He must know we will talk about this visit when we leave unless . . .' He paused, frowning, then shook his head.

'Unless . . . what?'

'Unless he's not going to let us leave.'

Gaye stiffened.

'He can't keep us forever. Garry, do talk sense.'

Garry sipped his drink.

'All right, but I don't like it. If Fennel and Ken weren't out there, I'd be worried. I'm going to talk to them.' He got up and went into his bedroom.

Gaye waited. She was also puzzled that Tak had taken them into the museum, but she wasn't worried. She told herself that Kahlenberg was so confident about his safety precautions, he didn't mind strangers seeing his museum.

Garry returned after some twenty minutes.

'Fennel agrees it looks suspicious. Themba has been left guarding the equipment. Fennel is coming here on his own, leaving Ken to keep watch. If Kahlenberg starts trouble, at least Ken can do something to help us. When we get the ring, we'll signal Ken and we'll all meet at the airfield and take off. We'll pick up Themba and get back to Mainville.'

'Do you think Kahlenberg will start trouble?'

'I'll tell you when I've met him,' Garry returned. 'How about another drink?'

At exactly 21.00 hrs., a Zulu servant came to take them to the main terrace.

Seated in his chair, Kahlenberg was waiting for them. He greeted them pleasantly and waved them to chairs near him.

'Tak tells me you are from *Animal World*, Miss Desmond.' he said, after Gaye had thanked him for receiving them. 'Have you been with them long?'

'Not very ... six months.'

'It is a magazine I take regularly. I am interested in animals. Why don't they give you a credit line, Miss Desmond?'

Watching, Garry was relieved to see Gaye was cool and seemed quite at ease. She laughed a little ruefully.

'I am one of the small fry, Mr. Kahlenberg. I do the routine work. I was hoping you would allow me to photograph this lovely house. I would get a credit for that.'

He studied her.

'I am afraid then you will have to wait a little longer for your credit. Photography is forbidden here.'

She met his blue-grey eyes, smiling.

'Even to me? I promise I will be most discreet and photograph only the house and the garden.'

'I am sorry.' He changed the subject by asking if she found his museum interesting.

'It is magnificent. I congratulate you.'

Three Zulus came silently on to the terrace and stood waiting before a beautifully laid table. At the same time, Hindenburg who had just finished his dinner, came slowly across the terrace to Kahlenberg.

'What a beauty!' Gaye exclaimed. 'May I stroke him?'

'It would be unwise,' Kahlenberg said, rubbing the cheetah's ear. 'My pet is a little uncertain with strangers ... even beautiful strangers, Miss Desmond.' He set his chair in motion and drove up to the table. 'Let us have dinner.'

When they were seated, Kahlenberg turned to Garry.

'And you, Mr. Edwards, have you been a professional pilot for long?'

Garry shook his head.

'Just started,' he said easily. 'Miss Desmond is my first client. Of course I've done a lot of chopper flying in the States, but I like a change, so I've set up business in Durban.'

'I see.'

Iced melons were served.

'You are after big game, Miss Desmond?'

'Yes. We were on our way to Wannock Game Reserve when I saw this wonderful house and I felt I had to see more of it. I do hope you don't think I was presumptuous.'

'Not at all. If I didn't wish you to be here, Tak would have sent you away. No, it is a pleasure to have such unexpected guests.'

'You are certainly out in the wilds . . . don't you find it lonely?' she asked.

'When one is as busy as I am, one hasn't time to feel lonely. It surprises me that you are a photographer.' Kahlenberg looked directly at her. 'I should have thought by the way you walk and by your appearance that you would have been a model.'

'I have done modelling, but I find photography more interest‑ing.'

'I too am interested in photography in an amateurish sort of way. I suppose you work entirely in colour?'

Gaye who had only the haziest knowledge of photography, realized they were getting on to dangerous ground.

'Yes, I work in colour.'

'Tell me, Miss Desmond . . .' Kahlenberg began when the second course of blue trout was served.

Gaye immediately began to enthuse about the fish, hoping to change the subject.

'It's my favourite fish,' she told him.

'How fortunate, but I was . . .'

Garry too had seen the red light and he tried to steer the conversation into another channel.

'Mr. Kahlenberg, I took a walk in your wonderful garden and came across a Zulu in full war dress . . . at least, I think it is war dress from what I've seen on the movies . . . a magnificent speci‑men.'

'Yes, I have over a hundred of these men,' Kahlenberg said. 'I like them to dress in their traditional costume. They are great hunters of beasts . . . and of men. They are the guardians of my estate. No one approaches here without being seen and

127

turned back. They patrol the surrounding jungle day and night in shifts.'

'Not the garden?' Garry asked casually as he could as he removed the back bone of the fish.

There was such a long pause that he glanced up to find Kahlenberg's eyes on him. The amused contempt in those eyes made Garry look quickly down at his fish.

'No, Mr. Edwards, they don't patrol the garden at night, but I have a few of them in the garden during the day when there are strangers here.'

'Well, they are certainly impressive,' Garry said, laying down his knife and fork. 'That was excellent.'

'Yes,' Kahlenberg absently reached out his hand and began to stroke Hindenberg's rough fur. The cheetah began to purr.

'What a marvellous sound,' Gaye exclaimed. 'Have you had him long?'

'A little over three years. We are inseparable.' Kahlenberg looked over at Garry. 'He is a magnificent watch-dog or I suppose I should say watch-cat. I had good proof of this a few months ago. One of my servants went mad and tried to attack me. He came into my office with a knife, but before he could even reach me, Hindenberg had literally torn him to pieces. The cheetah is the fastest moving animal on earth. Did you know that, Mr. Edwards?'

Garry eyed the cheetah and shook his head.

'He looks as if he could give a good account of himself.'

'He can.'

One of the waiters presented the main course which was a chicken browned in a casserole, the rib cage removed and the bird stuffed with diced lobster in a cream sauce, coloured by the coral of the lobster.

'Ah! This is something out of the ordinary,' Kahlenberg said. 'I got the recipe from one of the great Paris chefs. I think you will find it excellent.'

While the waiter was carving the chicken, Kahlenberg chatted agreeably, but both Gaye and Garry could see his mind was only half with them. He was obviously occupied with some business problem and wasn't giving them his entire attention.

The chicken was excellent as Kahlenberg had said it would be, and both of them expressed their appreciation.

Although the food was delicious, Gaye was relieved when the

meal was over. She found she had to work hard to hold Kahlenberg's interest. She was used to mixing with difficult people, but she mentally decided Kahlenberg was the stickiest host she had ever met. He was polite, but distant and she knew she had only half his attention. But she kept the conversation going, avoiding dangerous topics, asked questions about himself, discussed New York, Paris and London with him while Garry kept more or less silent, admiring her persistance.

As they were drinking coffee, Tak come out on to the terrace. He went up to Kahlenberg.

'Excuse me, sir, Mr. Vorster is on the telephone.'

Kahlenberg frowned.

'Oh, yes, I had forgotten. Tell him I will call back in five minutes.'

Tak bowed and went away.

'I must apologize, Miss Desmond, but I regret I will now have to leave you to your own devices. I have work to do. I doubt if we will meet again before you leave. I am sorry about the photographs. I hope you enjoyed your dinner.'

They got to their feet and both thanked him for his hospitality. He looked at them with an odd expression in his eyes, nodded, then set his chair in motion and drove off the terrace, followed by Hindenburg.

Reaching his office, he found Tak waiting for him.

'Thank you, Tak, those two were beginning to bore me. Lovely looking woman, of course, but a play thing.' He manoeuvred himself behind his desk. 'They are being watched?'

'Yes, sir.'

'Good. And the other three?'

'The guide no longer exists. Fennel and Jones are on the balancing rock watching through field glasses. They have been in contact with Edwards by two-way radio. Their conversation was intercepted. Fennel is coming here on his own, leaving Jones where he is. Edwards thinks we suspect him and is taking precautions.'

'Very wise of him. All right, Tak, you can go to your bungalow. I have some work to do, but intend to retire at my usual time. The rest of the staff can go.'

Tak hesitated.

'Is it wise, sir?'

'The guards will be here and Hindenberg. Yes, it is all right.'

Kahlenberg looked thoughtfully at Tak. 'It is much wiser that you don't have anything to do with this little affair. Good night.'

'Good night, sir,' and Tak went away.

Kahlenberg settled down to read a mass of papers that had come by the afternoon air delivery.

A little after half past ten, there came a soft tap on the door.

Frowning, he called, 'Come in.'

Kemosa entered.

'What is it?'

'Zwide, one of the gardeners, master, is dead.'

Kahlenberg raised his eyebrows.

'Dead? How did it happen? An accident?'

'I do not know, master. He complained of a headache and pains in his muscles. As he is always complaining, no one took any notice. Later he said his throat was on fire. A few minutes later, he fell down and died.'

'Extraordinary thing. Well, bury him, Kemosa. I dare say his wife will be pleased. He is no loss.'

Kemosa eyed his master, then bowed.

'I will have it done, master,' and he went out, closing the door softly behind him.

Kahlenberg sat back in his chair. A little smile that gave him a devilish expression lit up his face.

So the Borgia ring was lethal.

Chapter Eight

When Gaye and Garry returned to their suite, they found all the windows and the doors leading to the terrace closed and the air conditioner in operation.

Garry went immediately to the terrace doors and tried to open them, but they were securely locked and the key had been removed. When he tried to open one of the windows, he found it immovable.

'Battened down for the night,' he said, scratching his head. 'Now, how the hell is Fennel going to get in?'

'I thought you were being over optimistic. Is it likely they would leave all this open at night?' Gaye asked, sitting on the arm of a lounging chair. 'What are you going to do?'

'Alert Fennel. It's his job to get in. Maybe he can cope with this lock.' Garry looked at his watch. The time was 22.00 hrs. He sat down and looked across at Gaye. 'We have an hour to wait. What did you think of Kahlenberg?'

Gaye grimaced.

'I didn't like him. I think he was bored with me and a man who finds me boring can't expect to be my favourite person.' She laughed. 'What did you think of him?'

'He's dangerous,' Garry said soberly. 'I'll go further than that. I get the feeling, watching him, he isn't quite sane. I still have the idea we have walked into a trap. But as we're here, we'd be nuts not to have a go at the ring. I wonder if he was lying when he said the grounds weren't patrolled at night. I'll have to warn Fennel to be careful as he comes.'

'You don't think he's sane . . . what do you mean?'

'There's something about his eyes . . . I'm not saying he is mad, but off balance.'

'I'm sure you're imagining all this, Garry. I can't believe he could have let us see the museum if he really suspected us. I think he is soured by being a cripple, and if he was distant, then it was probably due to that . . . for all you know, he may be in pain.'

'You could be right,' Garry shrugged. 'But the whole set-up seems to me too easy.'

'Are you going to check on the elevator?'

'Of course. If it isn't working, I don't see how we can get at the door of the museum. I'll wait half an hour, then I'll go out and see.' He got up, crossed to the door and opened it. He looked down the deserted corridor. It was lighted, and in the far distance he could see the end of it terminating in double doors. 'No one about.' He returned to the lounge, closing the door. 'Could be tricky. If Tak or one of the servants come out of any of those rooms while I'm out there, I'm fixed. A fly couldn't hide out there.'

'You can always say you're walking in your sleep.'

Garry frowned at her.

'I wish you would take this more seriously. You don't seem to realize if we're caught we could be in a very nasty situation.'

'Let's worry about that if and when it happens.'

Garry suddenly grinned.

'I guess you're right. Come here and be kissed.'

She shook her head.

'Not now . . . we're working.'

He hesitated, then lighting a cigarette, he dropped into a chair.

'If we get away with this, what are you going to do with the money, Gaye?' he asked.

'Save it. I save all my money and invest it at six per cent in a Swiss bank. Soon, I'll have a nice income and then Shalik can look for another slave.'

'You don't like him?'

'Who would? He's useful, but that's all. And you, what are you going to do with your share?'

'Take a course in electronics,' Garry said promptly. 'I've always wanted to have an education, and up to now, I've never had the chance. With Shalik's money, I'll study, and then get myself a decent paying job. There are lots of opportunities in the electronics field.'

'You surprise me . . . you don't strike me as the studious type. Do you plan to get married?'

'Yes, but not until I've qualified. Then I will.'

'Got the girl lined up yet?'

He smiled at her.

'Yes, I think so.'

'Who is she?'

'No one you know . . . just a girl. We get along okay.'

'I rather thought you were going to say me.'

He laughed.

'You would have said no anyway.'

'Why are you so sure?'

'You would, wouldn't you?'

Gaye smiled at him.

'Yes. I wouldn't want to marry an electronics engineer. When I marry it will be a man who thinks big, lives big and is rich.'

'I know that. That's why I'm picking Toni.'

'Is that her name?'

Garry nodded.

'I wish you luck, Garry, and I hope you will be very happy with her.'

'Thanks. I hope you will be happy too, but don't pin too much on money.'

Gaye looked thoughtful.

'Life can be pretty rough without it.'

'Yes.' He stubbed out his cigarette and stared up at the ceiling. 'One's got to have enough, of course, but all this . . .' he waved his hand around the luxuriously furnished room. 'This isn't necessary.'

'It is to me.'

'That's where we differ.' He glanced at his watch. 'I guess I'll take a look at the elevator.'

Gaye got to her feet.

'I'll come with you. If we run into anyone, we can say we felt like a walk in the garden and as we couldn't get out through the terrace way we were going to try the front door.'

'A bit thin . . . but it'll have to do. Let's go.'

They moved silently out into the long corridor, paused to listen, heard nothing and then they walked fast down the corridor, passing the front door and on towards the hidden lift. Garry went to the window ledge and felt under it. His fingers found a button which he pressed. The wall slid back. They looked at each other, then motioning her to stay where she was, he approached the lift doors which swished silently open. He entered the cage, then first pressing the red button which Tak had told him turned off the alarm, he then pressed the green button. The doors closed and then the lift descended. When it reached ground level, Garry pressed the green button again and the lift ascended. He stepped into the corridor and reclosed the sliding wall.

Taking Gaye's hand in his, he ran silently down the corridor and back to their suite.

'Well, it works,' he said, closing the door. 'Now everything depends on whether Fennel can get in and then, of course, if he can open the door to the museum.'

After waiting a quarter of an hour, Garry picked up the two-way radio.

Fennel answered immediately.

Garry explained the situation and told Fennel the elevator was working. Fennel said there were still lights showing in the windows of the two extreme wings of the house.

'The light on the right is mine,' Garry said. 'The other light is from Kahlenberg's quarters.'

'The left wing light has gone out,' Fennel reported. 'The only light now showing is where you are.'

'Kahlenberg told me the grounds aren't patrolled, Lew,' Garry said, 'but I don't trust him. Take your time and use every scrap of cover as you come. There could be some of the Zulu guards around.'

'I'll watch it. I'll start now. It'll take me a good half-hour to get to you. Ken will remain here until we signal him.'

'Roger . . . out,' and Garry switched off. Turning to Gaye, he went on, 'He's on his way now. All the other lights have gone out.' He crossed to the bedside lamps and turned them on, then he turned off the ceiling lights. Going to the window, he peered into the darkness. The big moon was partially hidden by clouds, but after a few moments, his eyes became used to the darkness and he could make out the terrace furniture and beyond the beds of flowers.

'We could be flying back to Mainville in a couple of hours,' Gaye said. 'I'm going to change.'

She went into the bedroom, took off the sari and put on her shirt and shorts. When she returned to the lounge, she found Garry had also changed. They sat on the bed, looking through the window, waiting for Fennel.

The minutes dragged by. Both of them were keyed up as they sat, waiting. After what seemed an age, Garry put his hand on Gaye's arm.

'He's here.' He got to his feet and went to the window.

Fennel came out of the darkness and paused at the window and nodded. He lowered his tool kit to the ground and came to the terrace doors. With the aid of a pencil flash light, he examined the lock. Looking at Garry, he jerked up his thumb, then reached for his tool kit.

In a few minutes, the terrace doors swung open. Picking up his tool kit, Fennel moved into the lounge. He ignored Gaye as if she wasn't in the room. Turning to Garry, he said, 'Been doing yourself well, huh?' He looked around the room. 'Ken and I certainly caught the crappy end of this stick, didn't we?'

'Tough,' Garry said, smiling. 'Never mind. You'll recover.'

Fennel gave him an evil look, then turned away. Seeing the mood he was in, Gaye watched him, but didn't speak.

'Where's the lift?' Fennel asked. 'This job could take me three or four hours.'

Garry turned to Gaye.

'You'd better stay here if it's going to take that long.'

She nodded.

'All right.'

'How about the TV snoopers?' Fennel asked.

'They're there in the museum, but I've no idea where the monitor-room is or if anyone keeps watch at night.'

Fennel flushed with rage.

'Your job was to find out!' he snarled.

Garry went to the door, opened it and beckoned to Fennel.

'Take a look ... there are about thirty-five doors down that corridor. It could be behind any one of them. We can't walk in and check. Did you see any Zulus as you came through the garden?'

'No. What's that to do with it?'

'The chances are if they aren't patrolling the grounds, they don't keep watch at night on the TV monitor.'

'If they do, we're sunk.'

'There it is. Have you any ideas how we can check?'

Fennel thought, then shrugged.

'It could be anywhere ... could be in one of the huts away from the house.' He hesitated. 'It's taking a hell of a chance.'

'We either take the chance or we leave without the ring.'

'Will you take the chance?' Fennel demanded.

'Sure, if you will.'

'Then let's go.'

They moved silently into the corridor, leaving Gaye still sitting on the bed. A few minutes later, they were descending in the lift. When they reached the vaulted chamber, Garry pointed to the TV lens in the ceiling.

'There it is.'

Fennel moved under the lens and peered at it. Then he sucked in a deep breath.

'It's not operating.'

'Sure?'

'Yeah.'

Garry wiped his sweating hands on the seats of his shorts.

'There's the door to the museum. Do you want me to do anything?'

Fennel went to the door and examined the dial and the lock.

'No ... just leave it to me. It's going to take time, but I can get it open.' He opened his tool kit and laid out a selection of tools on the floor. Garry went over to a high-backed leather chair and sat down. He lit a cigarette and tried to contain his impatience.

Fennel worked carefully, whistling softly under his breath. His body concealed what he was doing, and after a while, Garry got bored watching his broad back, and getting up, he began to pace up and down. He smoked one cigarette after another and continually looked at his watch. After an hour had dragged by, he paused in his pacing to ask. 'How's it coming?'

'I've neutralized the time switch,' Fennel said, sitting back on his heels and wiping his forehead with his arm. 'That's the worst part of the job behind us. Now, I've got to tackle the lock itself.'

Garry sat down and waited.

Another hour dragged by, then Fennel gave a little grunt.

'I've done it!' he exclaimed.

Garry joined him at the door.

'Quicker than you thought.'

'Just luck. I've been five hours on one of these goddamn locks before now.' He stood up and pulled the door open. 'Do you know where the ring is?'

'I'll take you to it.'

Fennel hastily repacked his tool bag and together the two men moved into the picture gallery. Going ahead, Garry entered the second room and made for the lighted alcove. Then he paused, experiencing a sense of shock. The pedestal was there, but the glass box and the ring were missing.

'What is it?' Fennel demanded.

'It's gone!' Garry licked his dry lips. 'That's where it was ... it's gone! I thought ...'

He stopped short as he saw Fennel, his face twitching, was staring at the wide archway from which they had come into this room from the picture gallery.

Standing in the archway, wearing only leopard skins, were four giant Zulus, each holding a broad-bladed stabbing spear, their cruel, fierce black eyes fixed on the two startled men.

One of them said in guttural English. 'You come with us.'

'What they call a fair cop,' Garry said and moved towards the Zulus.

Fennel hesitated, but he knew they hadn't a chance against

these four giants. Cursing softly, he picked up his tool bag and moved after Garry.

As the minutes crawled by, Gaye became more and more uneasy and restless. She prowled around the luxurious lounge wondering how Fennel was getting on. It was now nearly two hours since they had left the lounge. She kept telling herself Fennel had said it might be a four hour job. She wished now she had gone with them. This long wait was getting on her nerves.

Then she heard a gentle tap on the door. Thinking it was Garry, she hastened across the lounge and opened the door. She was confronted by a Zulu who towered above her, the overhead light making his black skin glisten and the blade of his assigai flash.

She stifled a scream and stepped hurriedly back, her hand going to her mouth. The Zulu glared at her, his eyes like wet stones.

'You come with me,' he growled and stepped aside.

'What do you want?' Gaye asked, her voice husky with shock.

'The Master wants you . . . come!'

She hesitated. So Garry had been right after all, she thought, they had walked into a trap. By now she was recovering from her shock. There was nothing else to do but to obey, and lifting her head high, she walked out into the corridor.

The Zulu pointed to the double doors at the far end of the corridor with his assigai.

She knew it was useless to try to escape so she walked down the corridor, followed by the Zulu.

When she finally reached the double doors, they swung open automatically. Without looking at the Zulu, she walked into Kahlenberg's office, her heart thumping and her mouth dry.

At the far end of the vast room, Kahlenberg was sitting at his desk, a cigarette between his fingers, Hindenburg at his side.

'Ah, Miss Desmond,' he said, looking up. 'Please come and join me. I am watching something of great interest.'

As she moved around the desk, she saw the small TV set was on. Kahlenberg waved to a chair near his, away from Hindenburg who hadn't taken his eyes off her since she had entered the room.

'Sit down and look at this.'

She sat down, folding her hands in her lap and looked at the lighted screen. Her heart skipped a beat as she saw Fennel kneeling in front of the door leading to the museum.

'I believe he is actually defeating my beautiful lock,' Kahlenberg said. 'The makers assured me no one could do it.'

Fennel suddenly sat back on his heels.

'I've done it!' he exclaimed. His voice, slightly muffled, came through the speaker well enough.

Then Garry moved into the picture.

'Your friend is clever,' Kahlenberg said. Although he spoke mildly, his eyes glittered angrily. 'I didn't believe he could do it, but as you see, he has done it.'

Gaye said nothing.

'Usually, we immobilize the lift,' Kahlenberg went on, leaning back in his chair, his eyes still on the screen. 'But I was interested to see if this expert could break in. I will have to talk seriously with the makers. This won't do at all.'

They watched Fennel and Garry enter the museum. The picture changed to another angle as Kahlenberg reached forward and pressed a button on the set.

'I didn't want to alarm your friends so I didn't operate this set until they were satisfied it wasn't operating,' Kahlenberg went on. 'Now I fear they are in for a disappointment and a surprise.'

The picture showed the two men staring at the pedestal in the lighted alcove.

Gaye heard Fennel say, 'What is it?'

Leaning forward, Kahlenberg turned off the set.

'They will be here in a few minutes, Miss Desmond,' he said. He reached for a gold cigarette box and offered it. 'A cigarette?'

'Thank you.' Gaye took a cigarette and accepted a light.

'By the way, how is Mr. Shalik?'

If he had expected to startle her, he was disappointed. Her face was expressionless as she said, 'Last time I saw him, he seemed very well.'

'He continues to concoct his miserable little swindles?'

'I really don't know. He always seems to be busy, but just what he does I have no idea.'

'It is time he was stopped for good.' The flash of fire in Kahlenberg's eyes made her remember that Garry had thought this man was unbalanced. 'He is developing into a nuisance.'

'Do you think so? I should have thought he is no more of a nuisance than others,' Gaye said coolly. 'After all, Mr. Kahlenberg, surely you are birds of a feather?'

Kahlenberg's eyes narrowed slightly.

'What makes you say that, Miss Desmond?'

'Mr. Tak tells me everything in your museum is an original. I don't imagine the authorities of Florence would have sold you the Ghiberti panel or the Bernini David. I do know you stole the Borgia ring. Surely you are just as much a nuisance to the curators of various museums as Mr. Shalik is to you.'

Kahlenberg smiled.

'Yes, I admit everything in my museum has been stolen, but there is a reason. I appreciate beautiful things. I need beauty. I am too busy to visit Europe so I prefer to have my beauty here where I can see it when I have the inclination. But Shalik only plots for money, not beauty. He lives for money as I live for beauty. I intend to stop him.'

'Perhaps he needs the money,' Gaye said. 'You have more than enough. Perhaps you would be like Mr. Shalik if you had no money.'

Kahlenberg crushed out his cigarette. She could see he was controlling his temper only with an effort.

'You are a spirited woman, Miss Desmond. I am sure Mr. Shalik would be flattered to hear you defending him.'

'I am not defending him. I am just saying I see no difference between you and him,' Gaye said quietly.

At this moment the double doors swung open and Garry and Fennel walked in.

The four Zulus paused in the doorway, looking towards Kahlenberg who dismissed them with a wave of his hand. They stepped back and the doors closed.

'Come in, gentlemen and sit down,' Kahlenberg said, waving to chairs opposite his desk. 'As you see, Miss Desmond has already joined me.'

Garry went to a chair and folded himself down into it, but Fennel remained standing, glaring at Kahlenberg.

'Please sit down, Mr. Fennel,' Kahlenberg said quietly. 'Let me congratulate you. I didn't believe it was possible for anyone to open the door to my museum and yet you have done it. It is an achievement.'

'You can cut out the soft soap!' Fennel snarled. 'We came for the ring and we haven't got it so now we're getting the hell out of here and you're not stopping us!'

'Certainly you shall leave,' Kahlenberg said, 'but we have something to discuss first.'

'I'm not discussing anything with you!' Fennel snapped. He was livid with rage and disappointment. He looked at Gaye and Garry. 'Come on . . . he daren't stop us.' And he started towards the door, grabbed the handle but found the door locked. He spun around, glaring at Kahlenberg. 'Open this door or I'll break your goddamn neck!'

Kahlenberg raised his eyebrows.

'That could be dangerous for you, Mr. Fennel,' he said and made a soft clicking sound with his tongue against his teeth. Immediately, Hindenburg stood up and began to move slowly forward, his eyes on Fennel, his lips off his teeth in a ferocious snarl that made Fennel back away. 'I assure you,' Kahlenberg went on, 'my pet would tear you to pieces if I give him another signal. Sit down!'

Cowed by the cheetah, Fennel sat down abruptly by Garry.

'Thank you,' Kahlenberg said, then went on, 'I don't want the effort you three have made to get the Borgia ring to be wasted. As Miss Desmond has rightly pointed out, the ring doesn't legally belong to me. Since you all have shown so much initiative in getting as far as you have, I have decided to give you the ring on certain conditions.' He opened the drawer in his desk and took out the glass box, containing the ring. He placed the box on his desk where the three could see it.

Fennel glared at the ring and then looked at Garry.

'Is that it?' and when Garry nodded, Fennel turned to Kahlenberg. 'What do you mean . . . conditions?'

Kahlenberg addressed himself to Gaye.

'Miss Desmond, although I live in considerable luxury, although I am an exceedingly busy man, there are times when I get very bored with myself. As you see, I am a cripple. I am chained to this chair. One of my ambitions when young was to be a hunter. Nothing would have given me more satisfaction than to go on safari. But being a cripple, this has been impossible and I admit to a certain frustration. Any form of frustration to a man of my power and wealth is intolerable.'

'What the hell is this?' Fennel demanded impatiently. 'What are these conditions you are talking about?'

Kahlenberg ignored him.

'Here is the Borgia ring.' He picked up the glass box and handed it to Gaye. 'I understand each of you will be paid nine thousand dollars when you hand the ring to Shalik.' He smiled bleakly. 'You see, I have an excellent spy system. Nine thousand dollars to you is important money and naturally it will give you incentive to deliver the ring to Shalik.'

'You mean you are giving us the ring?' Fennel demanded.

'Miss Desmond already has it. I am now going to give you a further incentive . . . a much more important one . . . to deliver the ring to Shalik. But in spite of these two incentives, you still have to get the ring out of my estate.'

'So that's it,' Fennel's eyes narrowed. 'Your savages are going to stop us . . . is that it?'

'If they can they will. I am going to arrange a hunt. You three and Mr. Jones who is waiting for you will be the hunted and my Zulus will be the hunters. You must regard it as exciting a game as I shall. You will have a reasonable chance to escape the hunters because I am going to give you a three hour start. You will leave here at 04.00 hrs. when it will be light enough for you to make good speed and you will need good speed. At 07.00 hrs. my Zulus will come after you. It will be entirely up to your speed and ingenuity to avoid them.'

'Are you serious?' Garry asked.

'Certainly I am very serious as you will discover should you be unfortunate enough to be captured.'

'Suppose we are captured? What happens?'

Kahlenberg inclined his head.

'A sensible question, Mr. Edwards. If you are captured, you will be cruelly put to death. My men are extremely primitive. In the days of Shaka, the famous Zulu chief, when he caught his enemies, he had them impaled. This is done by hammering a sharpened skewer into the lower intestine and leaving the victim to die slowly and in extreme agony.'

Garry's face tightened.

'And your savages would do that to us if they caught us?' he asked.

'Yes, they would.'

There was a long pause, then Garry said, 'So you are staging this hunt to pander to your perverted, sadistic frustration. Is that it?'

Kahlenberg's face changed: from a courteous, mild spoken man he turned suddenly into a cruel, vicious looking lunatic.

'I am going to teach you not to trespass on my estate,' he said, leaning forward and glaring at Garry. 'You have dared to come here with your ridiculous tale and now you will pay for it!' He gained control of himself and sat back, his mouth working and he remained motionless until his rage died down. 'It is necessary to get rid of you all since you have seen my museum. It is essential that you don't escape to talk.'

A little shaken to realize that his idea that Kahlenberg was mentally unbalanced was now confirmed, Garry said, 'Then why give us the ring? Why not call your men in and kill us now?'

'The hunt will amuse me. You have the ring because if you do happen to escape, you deserve to keep it ... but I assure you, it is unlikely you will escape.'

'Suppose we give you our word not to talk and leave the ring with you?' Garry said. 'Would you allow us to use the helicopter and fly out?'

'No, and in case you are hoping to use your helicopter, I will tell you at once that it is under guard. Ten of my Zulus surround it and tomorrow early, one of my pilots will fly it back to the company you hired it from.' He pressed a button on his desk and a panel slid back on the opposite wall revealing a relief map of the estate and the house. 'I will give you a reasonable chance and I would be disappointed if the hunt were over in a few hours. I would like it to last several days. So please look at the map and study it. You will see the exit from the east is blocked by a range of mountains. Unless you are all expert rock climbers, I wouldn't advise you to go that way. I will warn you my Zulus think nothing of scrambling down the mountainside of these dangerous heights and they would quickly catch up with you. Nor would I recommend the exit to the south. As you can see from the map there is a river there, but what isn't shown is that the approaches to the river is swamp land and infested by crocodiles and some of the most deadly snakes in Natal. The north exit is straightforward. That is the way you came in. However, twenty of my Zulus are always guarding that approach. You didn't see them as you came in, Mr. Fennel, but they saw you and Mr. Jones and were continually reporting your progress. So I would advise you not to leave that way as although they let you in on my instructions, you may be sure they won't let you out. So this leaves only the west. It is not easy, but possible. You will find no water there, but there is a good jungle track that leads finally to the main highway to Mainville. It is some hundred and twenty kilometres and you would need to hurry. A Zulu can easily keep pace with a fast moving horse, but you do have a three hour start.' Kahlenberg looked at his watch. 'It is past my bed time. Please return to the guest suite and get a little rest. At 04.00 hrs. you will be released. Again I advise you to move as quickly as you can.' He pressed a button on his desk and the doors opened. The four waiting Zulus came in.

'Please go with these men,' Kahlenberg continued. 'There is an old African saying which you will all do well to remember. It is that the vulture is a patient bird. Personally I would prefer a vulture to one of my Zulus. Good night.'

Back in the guest suite and when Fennel closed the door, Garry said, 'He's a pathological case. I had a feeling about him the moment I saw him. Do you think he's bluffing about the Zulus?'

'No.' Gaye suppressed a shiver. 'He is a sadistic pervert. That expression on his face when he let the mask drop! Let's go now, Garry. They think the terrace doors are locked. We might gain seven hours if we leave at once.'

Garry went to the terrace doors and opened them. He paused, then stepped back, closing the doors.

'They are out there already . . . waiting.'

Gaye joined him and peered through the glass. She could see a half-circle of squatting Zulus, facing her: the moonlight glittered on their spears, their ostrich plumes moved in the slight breeze. Feeling frightened, she moved away from the doors and sat down.

'What are we going to do, Garry?'

'Are you any good on a mountain?' Garry asked, coming to sit by her side.

'I don't think so. . . . I've never tried.'

'You can cut the mountains out,' Fennel said, wiping his face with the back of his arm. 'I've no head for heights.'

'We'll have to consult Ken. We have to start north to pick Themba up. Without him, we're not going to get out.'

'That's right,' Fennel said. 'Ken says that the guy has a compass in his head. He'll get us out.'

'Let's have a drink.' Garry got to his feet and went over to the bar. 'What will you have, Gaye?'

'Nothing at this hour.'

'Lew?'

'Scotch.'

As Garry mixed the drinks, he asked, 'Has Ken got the Springfield with him?'

'No. We left it with Themba.'

'We could need it.'

'Yeah. We'll pick up Ken, and then go straight to where we left Themba. He's not only got the rifle, but extra water and most of the food. If we have to walk all the goddamn way, we could be at it for three or even four days.'

Garry saw Gaye was examining the ring through the glass of the box. He joined her and peered over her shoulder.

'Take it out and wear it,' he said. 'That box is awkward to carry and could get smashed. The ring will be a lot safer on your hand than in the box.'

'If anyone's going to wear it, it'll be me,' Fennel said, putting down his drink.

'She's wearing it,' Garry said quietly. 'I trust her, but I can't say I trust you.'

Fennel glared at him, but Garry's steady stare made him hesitate. Finally, he sat down with bad grace and picking up his glass, he drained it. Okay, you sonofabith, he thought. I'll fix you, when I fix her.

Gaye took the ring out of the box.

'The diamonds are lovely, but the ring isn't very beautiful, is it?' She tried the ring on the third finger of her right hand, but found it much too loose. 'Of course, I was forgetting ... it's a man's ring.' She slid it on her thumb. 'This is all right. It's a little awkward, but it won't come off.'

Garry looked at his watch. The time was 02.00 hrs.

'Go and lie down, Gaye. I'm going to my room. We want all the rest we can get. We don't know when we'll get our next sleep.'

He watched her go to her room, then he went to his, ignoring Fennel.

Fennel stretched out on the settee. He knew he wouldn't sleep. All his desire and frustration came back to him as he thought of Gaye.

If he had to follow her back to England, he told himself, he would get even with her. He had hoped to have found a chance of fixing her on the way back to Mainville, but they would have to keep moving if they were to shake off the Zulus. Fennel shifted uneasily. The thought of being hunted by a pack of Zulus dried his mouth.

A little before 04.00 hrs., Gaye was awakened by the sound of the beating of a drum. She sat up, swung her feet to the floor and listened.

Not far away, she could hear the rhythmic sound of the drum like a pulse beat. She looked hastily at her watch and saw it was two minutes to the hour. She snatched up her rucksack and went into the lounge.

Garry and Fennel were standing by the terrace doors.

A giant Zulu came across the terrace and beckoned to them. He was a magnificent specimen of a man in his leopard skin and ostrich plumes.

'Here we go,' Garry said and opened the terrace doors.

The drum beat now was very loud. A row of some thirty Zulus made a wall of glistening black bodies, covered with leopard skins. The ostrich plume head-dresses bobbed as they shuffled and stamped to the drum beat. They carried long narrow shields of buffalo hide and held in their left hands six throwing spears as they bent, straightened, shuffled and stamped. They made a frightening, awe-inspiring sight.

The lone Zulu made a savage gesture, jerking his assigai first at the three and then towards the distant jungle.

The two men slung their rucksacks on their shoulders and with Gaye between them, moved out on to the terrace.

At the sight of them the dancing men uttered a loud, savage growl that set Gaye's heart racing. The drum beat increased.

They walked quickly across the lawn, looking ahead and not at the Zulus. Gaye had to control herself not to run. They kept on, and in a few minutes, they were in the jungle.

'Nice looking lot,' Garry said. 'They are the boys who are coming after us. Where's Ken?'

Fennel pointed.

'See that balancing rock up there? That's where he is.' He cupped his hand to his mouth and bawled, 'Ken! Come on down, pronto!' Then taking out his flashlight, he turned it on and began waving it. A light signalled back from the rock and they heard Ken shout, 'I'm coming. Keep your light on.'

145

Five minutes later, he joined them.

'Did you get it? I thought you were going to the airfield.'

'We got it!' Fennel said. 'We've got to get to Themba fast. The chopper's out. Come on, I'll tell you as we go.'

Ken peered at him.

'Trouble?'

'I'll say ... get going!'

Ken started off with Fennel, talking, by his side. Garry and Gaye kept together.

When Ken understood the situation, he increased his pace.

'You really think they're coming after us?'

'Damn sure of it. I won't worry so much once I've got the rifle,' Fennel said. 'If they look like overtaking us, we can ambush them, but without the rifle we're in dead trouble.'

As they hurried along the jungle track, Garry was thinking of the best way to evade the Zulus. If they took the exit from the west which Kahlenberg had said was relatively easy, it would develop into a race between them and the Zulus who could move with the speed of a galloping horse. The east exit was out. None of them had any experience of mountain climbing whereas, according to Kahlenberg, the Zulus had. The north exit was too dangerous. Garry felt sure Kahlenberg had been speaking the truth when he had said he had men already posted there. That left the south exit ... swamps and crocodiles and possibly the last exit the Zulus would imagine they would try.

In around forty minutes, they reached the open space where they had left Themba. Twenty minutes less than it had taken Ken and Fennel to reach the balancing rock. They were all a little breathless and all jumpy.

'It's that tree over there,' Ken said pointing.

'You sure? He's not there.' Fennel stared across the open space in the dim light of the approaching dawn.

'Themba!' Ken shouted. 'Themba!'

The silence that greeted them sent a chill through them. Ken broke into a run. The others followed him.

Reaching the tree, Ken stopped. He knew it was the tree under which they had left Themba. Not only did he recognize the stunted thorn bush he had noticed when he had left with Fennel, but there was a heap of firewood piled by the tree. Under this tree had been their jerry can of water, the bag of food and the Springfield rifle. There was no sign of any of these things.

'The bastard's skipped with our stuff!' Fennel snarled.

'He wouldn't do that. Something's happened to him.'

It was Garry who spotted the grave away to his right.

'What's that?'

They looked at the mound of freshly turned earth and moving together, they approached it.

So there should be no mistake as to what lay under the soil, placed on top of it was Themba's Australian bush hat.

Ken was the first to realize what had happened.

'They killed him, and they've taken the food, the water and the rifle,' he said huskily.

For a long moment they all stood staring down at the grave.

Pulling himself together, Garry said, 'Well, we now know what to expect. We've got to get moving. Look, Ken, Fennel's told you about the four exits. I'm opting to go south. They'll expect us to go by the west exit. With luck, by going south and through the swamps, they may not be able to track us. What do you think?'

'It depends how bad the swamps are. They can be sheer hell, and that's crocodile country.'

'All the same, I think it's our best bet. Have you a compass?'

Ken produced a small compass from his pocket.

'I'm a qualified navigator,' Garry went on. 'Do you want me to lead the way or will you do it?'

'You do it. I've always relied on Themba.'

'Then we go south.' Garry steadied the compass and got a bearing. 'Let's go.'

He started along a track with Gaye at his heels. Fennel and Ken followed behind.

None of them said anything. Themba's death had shocked them all. The danger that was threatening them had been sharply brought home to them.

They moved at a fast pace. The time was now 04.50 hrs. In a little more than two hours the Zulus would be after them.

They had been walking for some twenty minutes when Garry stopped and checked the compass.

'This track's beginning to curve to the west,' he said as the other two came up. 'We'll have to leave it and cut through the jungle.'

They looked at the high tangled grass and the thorny shrubs and the trees.

147

'That's going to slow us up like hell,' Fennel complained.

'Can't be helped. We've got to go south and that's the way to the south.'

'I don't want to scare you,' Ken said quietly, 'but this is snake country. Keep your eyes skinned.'

Gaye clutched hold of Garry's arm.

'Don't worry,' he said, forcing a grin. 'I'll look after you. Let's go.'

They began to toil through the thick matted grass, zig zagging around the trees, aware of the chattering monkeys overhead.

Garry kept checking the compass. While Kahlenberg had been talking, Garry had been studying the wall map. He had realized that the river could be their salvation for he remembered as he flew over the estate, seeing the river in the distance and also seeing a small town to the south of it. The river was now vitally important to them as they had no water with them.

But he was also aware that since entering the jungle, their pace had slackened and he felt pretty sure the Zulus would have much less difficulty in covering this kind of ground than they were having.

After some three kilometres, they came out on to another jungle track which headed due south.

'How are you making out?' Garry asked, as he quickened his pace, catching hold of Gaye's hand and pulling her along with him.

'I'm all right, but I wish we knew how far we have to go.'

'I don't think it's too far ... around twenty kilometres before we get off the estate. I studied that wall map. This is the nearest exit to Kahlenberg's boundary.'

Plodding along behind, Fennel was being handicapped by the weight of his tool bag.

'I'll carry it for a bit,' Ken said, seeing Fennel was tiring.

Fennel stopped and regarded the bag angrily.

'No, you won't! I've had enough of this bloody thing. We'll never get anywhere if we go on carrying it. So okay, it cost me money, but if we get out of here I can buy a new kit. If we don't get out, then I won't need one. To hell with it.' He heaved the tool bag far into the jungle.

'I would have carried it,' Ken said.

Fennel grinned crookedly at him.

'I know and thanks. I'm glad to be rid of it.'

They stepped out and soon caught up with the other two. Then suddenly the track petered out into a large puddle of oozing mud.

'This is where the swamp starts,' Ken said. 'With the rain we've had, it could be bad.'

They left the track and moved into the jungle. The ground felt soft under their feet, but they pushed on. Later, the ground began to squelch under their weight and the going became harder.

By now the sun was up and they could feel the steamy heat. Garry kept checking the compass. When the ground got too sodden, they had to find a way around it and then get back on the compass bearing. The smell of rotting humus, the steamy heat that steadily increased as the sun climbed above the trees, the slippery boggy ground made progress slow and unpleasant.

They kept moving, their eyes searching the ground for snakes.

Ken said suddenly, 'They're on their way.'

Garry looked at his watch. The time was exactly 07.00 hrs. They all increased their pace with a feeling of slight panic, but the increase didn't last long: the going was too hard.

Ken said suddenly, 'I can smell water. The river's not far off.'

Ten minutes later, they came out of the shade of the trees to a broad, slippery bank leading down to a brownish stream, not more than twenty metres wide.

'That's our direction if we can get across,' Garry said. 'Think it's deep?'

'Could be.' Ken joined him and surveyed the water. 'It's no distance ... just the curse of getting wet in that foul water. I'll see.' He took off his shoes and shirt, padded across the oozing mud and grabbing hold of a branch of a tree, he lowered himself into the stagnant water while he groped to find bottom with his foot.

'It's deep. We'll have to swim.' He let himself go, then started across the stream to the other side of the bank with a strong, over-arm stroke.

It happened so quickly none of the other three watching him believed what they were seeing. There was a sudden rush from the thick jungle grass on the opposite bank. Something that looked like a green and brown tree trunk flashed into the water near Ken. An evil looking scaly snout revealed itself for a brief moment. Ken screamed and threw up his arms.

Then he and the crocodile vanished under the water which became agitated and rapidly turned into a foaming vortex of stinking brown water, horribly tinged with red.

Chapter Nine

At midday it rained. For the past two hours, swollen, black clouds had slowly built up, darkening the sky and blotting out the burning sun. The heat, by the placidly flowing stream, had become more and more oppressive. Then abruptly the rain came as if the sky had opened, releasing a deluge of warm water that soaked the three to the skin in seconds. So heavy was the rain, they were blinded by the water smashing down on them and were enveloped in steaming mist.

Catching hold of Gaye's hand, Garry ran into the jungle and paused under the cover of a vast baobab tree, its thick foliage offering a leaky shelter.

Cursing and muttering, Fennel joined them. They squatted down, their backs against the tree and stared at the now raging river in silence.

None of them had spoken for four hours. The shock of Ken's horrible end had reduced them to a numbed silence. Although they hadn't known him for long, they had all liked him for there had been nothing to dislike about him. What shocked them more than anything was the swiftness and the way of his going.

Gaye was sure that the terrible scene was now indelibly printed on her mind. Ken's terrified expression, his wild scream as the crocodile's teeth had crunched down on his leg and the brief sight of the evil, scaly snout were the ingredients of future nightmares.

Garry too had been violently shocked, but he was mentally much more resilient than either Gaye or Fennel. When he had seen Ken disappear and had seen the blood on the foaming water, he knew there was nothing he could do to help him. His duty to the others and himself was to keep moving, for he knew they dare not waste a moment, ever aware of Kahlenberg's threat that if caught, they would be impaled, and he had enough imagination to know such a death would be far more horrible than Ken's death. So catching hold of Gaye's hand, ignoring her hysterical sobbing, he dragged her away from the scene and back into the jungle. He kept moving until finally she steadied herself, stopped sobbing and continued with him, walking like a zombie.

Perhaps of the three of them, Fennel was the most affected. He had come to admire Ken. The episode with the Land Rover on the narrow track had enormously impressed him. He knew he hadn't the guts to have done such a thing. Ken's coolness when he was dangling at the end of the cable had completely wiped out Fennel's hostility. Ken's death now left him viciously angry, and in a brooding, homicidal state of mind. Why hadn't this son-ofabitch Edwards gone into the stream first? He and his whore weren't worth a tenth of what Ken had been worth. He looked at them out of the corners of his small glittering eyes. Garry had his arm around Gaye and Fennel felt a hot, furious rush of blood to his head. Well, I'll fix them, he thought. No one shoves me around as that bitch did without paying for it.

Garry was speaking quietly to Gaye.

'This rain's lucky. It'll wash out our tracks. This was the one thing I was praying for. They can't track us after this storm.'

Gaye clutched his hand. She was still too shocked to speak.

After some ten minutes, the rain began to slacken.

'We must get on,' Garry said, getting to his feet. 'We've got to cross the river.' He turned to Fennel. 'Think we could build a raft?'

'I've thrown my goddamn tool kit away,' Fennel told him. 'How the hell can we build a raft without tools?'

Garry walked to the edge of the river. The opposite bank was thick with high grass and shrubs. Were more crocodiles lurking on the bank, hidden from sight, waiting for them? After what had happened to Ken, he decided the risk was too great to attempt a crossing. He decided to push on down the river in the hope that they would come to a clearing where crocodiles couldn't conceal themselves.

'Before we go further, let's eat,' he said, and opening Ken's rucksack, he produced a can of stewed beef. 'We'll split this between the three of us.'

'I'm not hungry . . . I don't want any,' Gaye said listlessly.

'You've got to eat!' Garry said sharply. 'Now, come on.'

'No . . . leave me alone.'

Garry looked closely at her. Her white drawn face, her eyes that had become sunken, began to worry him.

'Are you all right?'

'I have a headache. The thought of food makes me feel ill . . . just leave me alone.'

Was it shock? he asked himself. Or was she ill? He flinched at the thought. To fall sick now would be a disaster.

The meal finished, the two men got to their feet. Garry went over to Gaye and touched her lightly on her shoulder. She opened her eyes, and again he felt a pang of alarm at the heavy, dull look in her eyes. She dragged herself to her feet.

'You're not ill, Gaye?' he asked.

'No.'

'Come on!' Fennel barked. 'I want to get going if you don't!'

Garry walked by Gaye's side. She moved listlessly and had lost the spring in her step. He took her arm.

'Don't fuss!' She tried to pull away. 'I'm all right. It's just this awful headache.'

He kept hold of her and walked on, but they weren't making the speed they had made earlier on.

'Keep moving for God's sake!' Fennel barked suddenly. 'What the hell are you two loitering for?'

Gaye made an effort and quickened her pace. They kept on, but after a couple of kilometres, she again began to lag and Garry found he had to force her on. He was seriously worried now. She seemed to be walking in her sleep, dragging one foot after the other.

'You're feeling rotten, aren't you?' he said at last. 'What is it?'

'My head feels as if it is going to burst . . . I suppose it's the sun.'

'Let's rest for a moment.'

'No . . . I'll manage. Just don't fuss.'

Another three kilometres brought them to a place Garry was hoping to find. The jungle fell away, either side of the river mud flats with no cover spread out before them.

'This is where we cross,' Garry said. He eyed the swift moving river. 'Do you think you can manage, Gaye?'

'Yes, if you keep near me.'

Fennel came to the edge of the bank and surveyed the water suspiciously.

'Are you going first?' he asked Garry.

'Don't get excited . . . it's safe enough and it's not far across,' Garry said curtly. He led Gaye to some shade. 'Sit down. I want to find a branch of a tree to get our stuff over dry.'

She sank down as Garry went off into the jungle.

Fennel eyed her, thinking all the glamour had gone out of her now.

'What the hell's the matter with you?' he demanded, standing over her.

She put her head in her hands.

'Leave me alone.'

'Are you sick?'

'I have a headache . . . leave me alone.'

The sunlight reflected on the diamonds of the Borgia ring, making them sparkle. Fennel eyed the ring.

'You better give me the ring to carry. I don't want it lost. Come on, give it to me!'

'No!'

Garry came out of the jungle dragging a long branch covered with foliage behind him.

Muttering under his breath, Fennel moved away from Gaye.

It took Garry very few minutes to tie the rucksacks and their shoes to the branch.

'Let's go,' he said to Gaye. 'Hang on to the branch. I'll push it over.'

Uneasily, Fennel watched them enter the water. He looked up and down the opposite bank, expecting to see a crocodile appear, but saw nothing. They were across in a few minutes, and his eyes narrowed when he saw Gaye had collapsed on the mud bank and lay face down. He entered the water and swam fast and in panic to the other side.

Garry had turned Gaye and was kneeling over her, looking anxiously down at her white face. She seemed unconscious.

Water streaming from him, Fennel came up.

'What's the matter?' he demanded roughly.

'She's ill.' Garry picked up the unconscious girl and carried her across the mud flat into the shade of a tree. He laid her down on a carpet of rotting leaves. 'Get the rucksacks and the shoes,' he went on.

Fennel did as he was told, put on his shoes and came back to where Garry was anxiously watching Gaye.

'I guess she's picked up some bug,' Fennel said indifferently. 'Well come on, Edwards, let's go. Those black bastards may be right behind us.'

'Look around and see if you can find two straight branches. We could make a stretcher with our shirts.'

Fennel stared at him.

'You out of your head? Do you imagine I'm going to help carry that bitch through this goddamn jungle and in this heat when those blacks are racing after us? You carry her if you want to, but I'm not.'

Garry looked up at him, his face hardening.

'Are you saying we should leave her here?'

'Why not? What's she to us? You're wasting time. Leave her and get going.'

Garry stood up.

'You go. I'm staying with her. Go on . . . get out!'

Fennel licked his lips as he stared at Garry.

'I want the compass and the ring,' he said softly.

'You get neither! Get out!'

For a man of his bulk, Fennel could move very quickly. His fist flashed out as he jumped forward, but Garry was expecting just this move. He ducked under the fist and hooked Fennel to the jaw: a crushing punch that flattened Fennel.

'I said get out!' Garry snapped.

Fennel had landed on his back, his arms flung wide. His groping fingers closed on a rock, half-hidden in the grass. He gripped it and with a violent movement, hurled it at Garry. The rock smashed against the side of Garry's head and he went down as if he had been pole-axed.

His jaw throbbing, Fennel struggled to his feet. He approached Garry cautiously and bent over him. Satisfied that Garry was unconscious, Fennel slipped his fingers into Garry's shirt pocket and found the compass. He crossed over to where Gaye was lying. Catching hold of her right wrist, he pulled the Borgia ring off her thumb. As he did so, she opened her eyes and seeing his face close to hers, she struck at him with her left hand.

It was such a feeble blow Fennel scarcely felt it. He grinned viciously.

'Good-bye, baby,' he said, bending over her. 'I hope you suffer. I'm taking the compass and the ring. You two will never get out of here alive. If you had been nice to me, I would have been nice to you. You asked for it and you're getting it.' He stood up. 'If the Zulus don't find you, the vultures will. So long, and have a wonderful time while it lasts.'

Gaye closed her eyes. He doubted if she had understood half what he had said, but it gave him a lot of satisfaction to have said it.

He picked up the rucksack containing the last of the food and the water bottle, checked the compass for his bearing, then set off fast into the dark steamy heat of the jungle.

Garry stirred and opened his eyes. A shadow passed over his face, then another. He looked up at the tree. He could see through the foliage, heavy grey clouds moving sluggishly westward. Then he saw two vultures settling heavily on the topmost branch of the tree, bearing it down under their combined weight. Their bald, obscene looking heads, the cruel, hooked beaks and their hunched shoulders sent a chill of fear through him.

His head throbbed and when he touched the side of his face, he felt encrusted blood. He was still dazed, but after resting a few minutes, his mind began to clear. His hand went to his shirt pocket and he found the compass gone. He struggled to his feet and went unsteadily over to where Gaye was lying. She now looked flushed and her forehead was covered with beads of sweat. She seemed to be either sleeping or unconscious. He looked at her right hand. It was no surprise to see the ring was missing.

He squatted down beside her and considered his position. He had possibly fifteen kilometres of jungle swamp ahead of him before he reached the boundary exit. He glanced towards the rucksacks and saw the rucksack containing the food was also missing. Without food or water, he couldn't hope to last long. His watch told him it was 16.00 hrs. The Zulus had been searching for them now for nine hours. Had the rain washed out their tracks? If it hadn't, he could expect the Zulus to appear any time now.

Had he been alone, he would have gone off at once in the hope of overtaking Fennel, but he couldn't leave Gaye.

He looked down at her. Maybe Fennel had been right about her picking up a bug. She looked very ill and was obviously running a high temperature. As he watched her she slowly opened her eyes. It took her a few moments to get him into focus, then she frowned, moving as if in pain.

'You're hurt,' she said huskily.

'It's all right.' He took her hot hand in his. 'Don't worry about that.'

'He's taken the compass and the ring.'

'I know. Take it easy. Don't worry about anything.'

The sudden crashing of branches overhead startled them and both looked up. One of the vultures had dropped from the upper branch to a lower one and was stretching its mangy neck, peering down at them.

Getting to his feet, Garry picked up the blood-stained rock and heaved it up the tree. The rock whistled by the vulture. It flew off with a great flapping of wings and rustling of leaves.

'It knows I am dying,' Gaye said, her voice breaking. 'Garry! I'm so frightened.'

'You're not dying! You've caught a bug of some sort. In a day or so, you'll be fine.'

She looked at him, and his heart sank at the fear and hopelessness he saw in her eyes.

'There's nothing you can do for me,' she said. 'Leave me. You must think of yourself, Garry. It won't be long for me. I don't know what it is, but it's as if something is creeping up inside me, killing me piecemeal. My feet are so cold, yet the rest of me burns.'

Garry felt her naked feet. They were ice cold.

'Of course I'm not leaving you. Are you thirsty?'

'No. I have no feeling in my throat.' She closed her eyes, shivering. 'You must go, Garry. If they caught you . . .'

It dawned on him then that she could be dying. With her by his side, the attempt to get through the jungle wouldn't have daunted him, but realizing he might have to do it alone sent a prickle of panic through him.

'Do you believe in God?' she asked.

'Sometimes.'

He hesitated.

'For both of us this is really the time to believe, isn't it?'

'You're going to be all right.'

'Isn't it?'

'I guess so.'

There was a sudden disturbance in the tree above them as the vultures settled again.

She caught hold of his hand,

'You really mean you are going to stay with me?'

'Yes, darling. I'm staying.'

'Thank you, Garry, you're sweet. I won't keep you long.' She looked up at the vultures who were looking down at her. 'Promise me something.'

'Anything.'

'You won't be able to bury me. You can't dig with your bare hands, darling, can you? Put me in the river, please. I don't mind the crocodiles, but the vultures . . .'

'It's not coming to that. You rest now. By tomorrow, you'll be fine.'

'Promise, Garry.'

'All right, I promise, but . . .'

She interrupted him.

'You were right when you told me not to pin everything on money. If money hadn't meant so much to me I wouldn't be here now. Garry, have you a piece of paper and a pen? I want to make my will.'

'Now, look, Gaye, you've got to stop being morbid.'

She began to cry helplessly.

'Garry . . . please . . . you don't know what an effort it is even to talk. I hurt so inside. Please let me make my will.'

He went to his rucksack and found a notebook and a biro.

'I must do it myself,' she said. 'The manager of the Swiss bank knows my handwriting. Prop me up, Garry.'

As he raised her and supported her, she caught her breath in a sobbing moan of pain. It took her a long time to write the letter, but finally it was done.

'Everything I have, Garry darling, is for you. There's over $100,000 in securities in my numbered account in Bern. Go and see Dr. Kirst. He's the director there. Tell him what has happened . . . tell him everything and especially tell him about Kahlenberg's museum. He'll know what to do and keep you clear. Give him this will and he will arrange everything for you.'

'All right . . . you're going to be all right, Gaye. Rest now,' and Garry kissed her.

157

Three hours later, as the sun, a red burning ball in the sky, sank behind the trees, Gaye drifted out of life into death. With the deadly scratch she hadn't noticed, the Borgia ring claimed yet another victim.

Fennel had been walking fast now for the past two hours. From time to time, swamp land had made him take a wide detour, wasting time and energy. Once he had floundered up to his knees in stinking wet mud when the ground had given under his feet. He had had a desperate struggle to extricate himself: a struggle that left him exhausted.

The silence in the jungle, the loneliness and the heat all bothered him but he kept reassuring himself that he couldn't now be far from the boundary exit and then his troubles would be over.

He kept thinking of the triumphant moment when he would walk into Shalik's office and tell him he had the ring. If Shalik imagined he was going to get the ring for nine thousand dollars, he was in for a surprise. Fennel had already made up his mind he wouldn't part with the ring unless Shalik paid him the full amount the other three and he would have shared . . . thirty-six thousand dollars. With any luck, in another four or five days, he would be back in London. He would collect the money and leave immediately for Nice. He was due a damn good vacation after this caper, he told himself. When he was tired of Nice, he would hire a yacht, find some bird and do a cruise along the Med., stopping in at the harbours along the coast for a meal and a look around: an ideal vacation and safe from Moroni.

He had now dismissed Gaye and Garry from his mind, never doubting he had seen the last of them. The stupid, stuck-up bitch had asked for trouble. No bird ever turned him down without regretting it. He wished Ken were with him. He frowned as he thought of the way Ken had died. With Ken, he would have felt much more sure of himself. Now, the sun was going down and the jungle was getting unpleasantly dark. He decided it was time to stop for the night. He hurried forward, looking for a clearing where he could get off the narrow track. After some searching, he found what he was looking for: a patch of coarse grass, clear of shrubs with a tree under which he could shelter if it rained.

He put down his rucksack and paused to wonder if he dare light a fire. He decided the risk was negligible and set about gathering sticks and kindling. When he had collected a large heap by the tree, he got the fire going, then sat down, his back resting against the tree. He was hungry and he opened the rucksack and took stock. There were three cans of stewed steak, two cans of beans and a can of steak pie. Nodding his satisfaction, he opened the can of steak pie. When he had finished the meal, he lit a cigarette, threw more sticks on the fire and relaxed.

Now he was sitting still, he became aware of the noises in the jungle: soft, disturbing and distracting sounds: leaves rustled, some animal growled faintly in the distance: Fennel wondered if it were a leopard. In the trees he could hear a sudden chatter of hidden monkeys start up and immediately cease. Some big birds flapped overhead.

He finished his cigarette, added more sticks to the fire and stretched out. The dampness had penetrated his clothes and he wondered if he would sleep. He closed his eyes. Immediately, the distracting sounds of the jungle became amplified and alarming. He sat up, his eyes searching beyond the light of the fire into the outer darkness.

Suppose the Zulus had spotted the fire and were creeping up on him? he thought.

They hammer a skewer into your lower intestine, Kahlenberg had said.

Fennel felt cold sweat break out on his face.

He had been crazy to have lit the fire. It could be spotted from a long distance away by the sharp-eyed savages. He grabbed up a big stick and scattered the fire. Then getting to his feet, he stamped out the burning embers until the sparks had died in the wet grass. Then it was even worse because the darkness descended on him like a hot, smothering, black cloak. He groped for the tree, sat down, resting his back against it and peered fearfully forward, but now it was as if he were blind. He could see nothing.

He remained like that for more than an hour, listening and starting with every sound. But finally he began to nod to sleep. He was suddenly too exhausted to care.

How long he slept, he didn't know, but he woke with a start, his heart racing. He was sure he was no longer alone. His built-in instinct for danger had sounded an emergency alarm in his mind. He groped in the darkness and found the thick stick with which he had scattered the fire. He gripped it while he listened.

Quite close ... not more than five metres from him, there was a distinct sound of something moving through the carpet of leaves. He had his flashlight by him and picking it up, his racing heart half suffocating him, he pointed the torch in the direction of the sound, then pressed the button.

The powerful beam lit up a big crouching animal that Fennel recognized by its fox-like head and its filthy fawn and black spotted fur to be a fully grown dog hyena.

He had only a brief glimpse of the animal before it disappeared into the thicket on the far side of the track, but that glimpse was enough to bring Fennel to his feet, panic stricken.

He remembered a conversation he had had with Ken while they were in the Land Rover on the first easy leg of the journey to Kahlenberg's estate.

'I get along with all the animals out here except the hyena,' Ken had said. 'He is a filthy brute. Not many people know this scavenger has the most powerful teeth and jaws of any animal. He can crack the thigh of a domestic cow the way you crack a nut. Besides being dangerous, he is an abject coward. He seldom moves except by night, and he will go miles following a scent and has infinite patience to wait to catch his prey unawares.'

With his eyes bolting out of his head, his hand shaking, Fennel played the beam of the flashlight into the thicket. For a brief moment he saw the animal glaring at him, then vanish.

He has infinite patience to wait to catch his prey unawares.

Fennel knew there was no further sleep for him that night, and he looked at his wristwatch. The time was 03.00 hrs. Another hour before it began to get light and he could move. Not daring to waste the battery, he turned off the flashlight. Sitting down, he leaned against the tree and listened.

From out of the darkness came a horrifying, maniacal laugh that chilled his blood and raised the hairs on the nape of his neck. The horrible, indescribably frightening sound was repeated ... the howl of a starving hyena.

Fennel longed for Ken's company. He even longed for Garry's company. Sitting in total darkness, knowing the stinking beast might be creeping slowly on its mangy belly, his powerful jaws slavering, towards him, he remained motionless, tense and straining to hear the slightest sound. He remained like that, his body aching for sleep, his mind feverish with panic for the next hour.

Whenever he dozed off, the howl of the hyena brought him awake and cursing. If only he had the Springfield or even an assigai, he thought, but he had nothing with which to defend himself except the thick stick which he was sure would be useless if the beast sprang at him.

When dawn finally came, Fennel was almost a wreck. His legs were stiff and his muscles ached. His body cried out for rest. He dragged himself upright, picked up his rucksack, and after assuring himself there was no sign of the hyena, he set off along the jungle track, again heading south. Although he forced himself along, his speed had slowed and he wasn't covering the ground as he had the previous day. He wished he knew how much further he had to go before he reached the boundary exit. The jungle was as dense as it had been yesterday and showed no sign of clearing. He walked for two hours, then decided to rest and eat. Sitting on a fallen tree, he opened a can of beans and ate them slowly, then he took a small drink from the water bottle. He smoked a cigarette, reluctant to move, but he knew he was dangerously wasting time. With an effort he got to his feet and set off again. Having walked for some five kilometres, he paused to check the compass. From the reading, he realized with dismay that he was now walking south-west instead of due south. The track had been curving slightly, taking him away from his direction and he hadn't noticed it.

Cursing, he fixed his bearing and saw that to move in the right direction, he would have to leave the path and force his way through the thick, evil smelling undergrowth. He hesitated, remembering what Ken had said about snakes.

It would be a hell of a thing, he thought, to have got this far and then to get bitten by a snake. Gripping his stick, he moved into the long, matted grass, feeling the sharp blades of the grass scratching at his bare legs. The sun was coming up, and already the heat was oppressive. The going was deadly slow now, and sweat began to stream off him as he slashed his way through the grass and tangled undergrowth with his stick, cursing aloud. Ahead of him, after a kilometre of exhausting struggle, he saw a wide open plain and he gasped with relief. He broke through to it, but almost immediately, his feet sank up to his ankles in wet, clinging mud and he backed away, returning to the undergrowth. The plain he had imagined would be so easy to cross was nothing more than a dangerous swamp. He was now forced to go around the swamp, making an exhausting detour, feeling his strength slowly ebbing from him as he struggled on in the breathless heat.

He now began to wonder if he would ever get out of this hellish place. He would have to rest again, he told himself. That was the trouble. He was worn out after a sleepless night. Maybe if he could sleep for three or four hours, he would get back his strength which he had always taken for granted and relied on.

It was a risk, he thought, but a risk that had to be taken if he was to conserve his strength for the last lap through the swamp. He remembered Ken had said hyenas only hunted at night. The beast was probably miles away by now. He would have to find somewhere to hide before he dare have the sleep his body was aching for. He dragged himself on until he saw a big, fallen tree some way from the track and surrounded by shrubs. This seemed as good a place as any, and when he reached it he found the ground on the far side of the trunk reasonably dry. Thankfully, he lay down. He made a pillow of his rucksack, placed the rucksack of food near at hand and the thick stick by his side. He lowered his head on the rucksack, stretched out and in a few moments, he was asleep.

He hadn't been sleeping for more than a few minutes when out of the jungle came the hyena. It sniffed the ground, paused, then cocked its head on one side as it eyed the fallen tree. Making a silent, wide detour, it slunk around to the other side of the tree where Fennel was sleeping.

The hyena hadn't eaten for two days and it was half mad with hunger, but although there was a meal before it for the taking, it was too cowardly as yet to attack. It sank down, its muzzle resting on its paws and stared with gleaming red eyes at the sleeping man.

Unhappily for Fennel, he was so exhausted, he slept the sleep of the dead, neither making a sound nor moving. After half an hour of watching the hyena finally convinced itself that there was no danger for a hit and run attack.

It hunched its hind legs, lifted itself and struck.

Fennel was awakened by such intense pain that he was screaming out as he opened his eyes. He half started up, but the pain raging in his legs absorbed all his strength and he fell back, his fists pounding the sides of his head as the rising pain drove him frantic. Looking down, he was horrified to see that where his right calf had been there was now only a mess of blood and splintered bone. He could even see the white of his shin bone where the fleshy part of his calf had been ripped away.

Sobbing and moaning, he looked frantically around and he saw the hyena some ten metres from him, its muzzle bloodstained as it chewed the lump of flesh.

Blood was pouring from the terrible wound and Fennel realized if someone didn't come to his help at once, he would be dead in a few minutes. Already faintness was gripping him. Gathering his remaining strength, he yelled, 'Help!' at the top of his voice.

The shout echoed through the jungle. Startled, the hyena dashed into the undergrowth and released its horrible laughing howl.

Fennel tried to shout again, but only succeeded in making a croaking sound that carried no distance. The agony raving through his body brought unconsciousness near. The blood pouring from his wound attracted a swarm of flies which were now excitedly buzzing around the fast growing pool of blood.

Fennel was now too weak to do anything but lie flat, shuddering and moaning with pain. He could see outlined against the grey clouds, a number of vultures circling overhead. He watched them drop into a nearby tree one by one and peer down at him speculatively.

He didn't see the hyena creeping on its belly towards him. He was only aware of it when he felt a sudden rush, smelt decay as the beast pounced on him, then a blinding pain as the sharp, powerful jaws and teeth bit through the top of his shorts and disembowelled him.

Ngomane, a magnificently built Zulu, had once worked on the Kahlenberg estate, but there had been woman trouble and he had been dismissed.

Before his dismissal, Ngomane had been one of the forty guards patrolling the jungle on the look-out for unwelcomed visitors and poachers. He knew the jungle as he knew the back of his hand and after his dismissal, he pondered how he could earn a living. He decided that as there were many crocodiles on Kahlenberg's estate and as he knew where to find them and as the other guards were sympathetic about his dismissal, it would be safe and profitable, from time to time, to kill a few of the reptiles and sell their skins to the white storekeeper in Mainville who never asked questions and paid well.

Ngomane was trotting silently along the jungle track, having just entered from the south boundary and was heading for the river, when he heard Fennel's frantic cry for help. He stopped abruptly, fingering his ancient rifle, looking uneasily in the direction of the sound. Then curiosity getting the better of caution, he moved into the jungle and in a few moments he had found what was left of Fennel.

Garry walked slowly along the river bank, keeping in the shade where possible, his eyes searching the ground before him for snakes and signs of hidden crocodiles.

He had decided that without a compass it would be inviting disaster to attempt to reach the boundary exit through the jungle. He remembered that the relief map in Kahlenberg's office had shown that after the river had passed the boundary of the estate, it continued on for some twenty kilometres to pass through a small town. Although he would be faced with a walk at least twice as long as the direct south route through the jungle, he knew if he could keep going, he could not lose his way and with any luck would not encounter swamp land and be forced to make exhausting detours.

On the other hand he exposed himself to attack from crocodiles and he could be more easily spotted if the Zulus had got this far up the river. But weighing the pros and cons, he finally opted for the river route.

He was feeling depressed and weary. He had committed Gaye's body to the river and had watched it float away into the darkness. He had hated the task, but he had no tool to dig a grave. Having seen her on her way, he had gone into the jungle and laid down. He had slept badly, dreaming of her and had started his walk soon after 05.00 hrs.

He had been walking now for four hours, not moving quickly, but steadily, carefully pacing himself to conserve his strength. He was hungry and thirsty. From time to time, he moistened his lips with the foul river water, but refrained from drinking it. He had four packs of cigarettes in his rucksack, and by continually smoking, he took the edge off his hunger and kept the mosquitoes at bay.

As he walked, he wondered how far Fennel had got by now. By the time he himself reached Mainville – if he ever reached it – Fennel would be on his way to Johannesburg. Garry was sure Fennel would immediately fly to London, hand over the ring, collect his share and then disappear. Garry wondered if Shalik would pay him his share once Shalik had the ring: he probably wouldn't. It didn't matter, Garry told himself. Thanks to Gaye, he was now worth $100,000. With such sum, he could take the course in electronics and then buy himself a partnership. But first he had to get back to England.

He rested at midday for an hour and then continued on. By dusk, he had covered twenty-five kilometres. By keeping to the river, the walk, except for the gnawing pangs of hunger and a raging thirst, had been far less arduous than if he had taken to the jungle, but he knew he had at least another thirty kilometres to face the following morning and he, like Fennel, began to wonder if he would make it.

He moved into the jungle when it became too dark to see where he was going and laid down under a tree and slept. He woke soon after 05.00 hrs. as the sun was beginning to rise. Going down to the edge of the river, he scooped the brown dirty water over his face and head and moistened his lips without swallowing. The temptation was great, but he resisted it, sure that the water could contain a host of deadly bacteria.

He started off, keeping his pace steady, heading for an elbow bend in the river, and wondering what he would find around the corner. With luck, he told himself, he could be at the exit of the estate.

It took him an hour to reach the bend and to get a clear view of the river which was now wide and straight. As he paused to examine both banks of the river, he suddenly stiffened. Could that be a boat pulled up on the mud flat some sixty metres ahead of him or was it a fallen tree?

He started forward, peering into the half light, and in a few minutes, he decided that it was a flat bottom canoe.

His hunger and thirst forgotten, his heart pounding, he broke into a stumbling run. He reached the canoe and then stopped abruptly.

Lying in the bottom of the canoe was a dead Zulu. By his side were two rucksacks which Garry recognized as belonging to Ken and Fennel and more welcome still, Ken's water bottle.

On the Zulu's forefinger of his right hand, flashing in the sunlight, was the Caesar Borgia ring.

As soon as Garry had cleared the customs at London Airport, he hurried to a telephone box and dialled Toni's number. The time was 10.25 hrs. and he was pretty sure she would be still sleeping. After the bell had rung for some minutes, he heard a click, then a sleepy voice said, 'Miss White is away.'

Knowing she was about to hang up, Garry shouted, 'Toni! It's me!'

There was a pause, then Toni, now very much awake, released a squeal of excitement. 'Garry! Is that really you, darling?'

'Yes. I've just got in from Jo'burg.'

'And you're calling *me*? Oh, darling! So she isn't so marvellous after all?'

'Don't let's talk about her.' Garry's voice went down a note. 'Listen, Toni, how are you fixed? I'm flying to Bern tomorrow morning and I want you to come with me.'

'Bern? Where's Bern?'

'It's in Switzerland. Didn't you learn anything at school?'

'I learned to make love. Who cares where Bern is anyway? You want me to come with you? Why, darling, of course! I'd go with you to Vierwaldstattersee if you wanted me to.'

'That's nice. Where's that?'

She giggled.

'It's in Switzerland too. How long will we be staying?'

'A day or so, then I thought we would go down to Capri for two weeks and really live it up. You know where Capri is, don't you?'

'Yes, of course. I'd love to, Garry, but I simply can't. I have to work. I can manage three days, but not two weeks.'

'Wives shouldn't work, Toni.'

There was silence. He could hear her breathing over the line and he imagined her kneeling on the bed in her shortie nightdress, her big blue eyes very round and astonished, and he grinned.

'Did you say *wives* shouldn't work?' she asked, her voice husky.

'That's what the man said.'

'But I'm not married, Garry.'

'You soon will be. See you in two hours from now,' and he hurriedly hung up.

He piled his luggage into a taxi and told the driver to take him to the Royal Towers Hotel.

Arriving at the hotel, he had his luggage put in the baggage room and then asked the hall porter to call Shalik's suite and announce him.

There was a brief delay, then the hall porter told him to go up.

Arriving at the suite, he tapped and entered the outer room. A blonde girl sat at the desk, busily typing. She surveyed him as she paused in her work and got to her feet. Dressed in black, she was tall and willowy and exactly the type of girl Garry went out of his way to avoid: hard, shrewd, intelligent and very efficient.

'Mr. Edwards?'

'Correct.'

'Mr. Shalik will see you now.' She opened the door to Shalik's office and motioned him forward as if she were shooing in a nervous chicken.

Garry smiled at her more from force of habit than to be friendly. He need not have bothered. She wasn't looking at him and her indifference irritated him.

He found Shalik sitting at his desk, smoking a cigar, his plump hands resting on the blotter.

As Garry walked towards him, he said, 'Good morning, Mr. Edwards. Have you the ring?'

'Yes, I have it.' Garry sat down in the lounging chair opposite Shalik. He crossed his long legs and regarded Shalik.

'You have? My congratulations. I take it the other three will be coming to join us in a moment or so?'

Garry shook his head.

'No, they won't be coming to join us.'

Shalik frowned.

'But surely they want their fee?'

'They won't be coming and they won't be collecting their fee.'

Shalik sat back, studied the end of his cigar, then looked hard at Garry.

'And why not, Mr. Edwards?'

'Because they are dead.'

Shalik stiffened and his eyes narrowed.

'Are you telling me Miss Desmond is dead?'

'Yes, and so are the other two.'

Shalik made an impatient movement which conveyed he wasn't interested in the other two.

'But what happened?'

'She caught a bug . . . lots of dangerous bugs in the jungle, and she died.'

Shalik got to his feet and walked over to the window, turning his back to Garry. The news shocked him. He disliked strangers knowing that he was capable of being shocked.

After a few moments, he turned and asked, 'How do I know you are telling me the truth, Mr. Edwards? How did the other two die?'

'Jones was eaten by a crocodile. I don't know what happened to Fennel. He was probably killed by a Zulu. I found the Zulu dead with Fennel's rucksack and the ring. Fennel had stolen the ring and my compass and left Gaye and me to find our way out of the jungle. I succeeded: Gaye didn't.'

'Are you quite sure she is dead?'

'I'm sure.'

Shalik sat down. He wiped his damp hands on his handkerchief. He had an important assignment involving a million dollars lined up for Gaye when she returned. Now, what was he to do? He felt a bitter rage seize him. He would have to start another long and difficult search for a woman to replace her, and in the meantime, the assignment would fall through.

'And the ring?' he said, controlling his rage.

Garry took a matchbox from his pocket and pushed it across the desk to Shalik who picked it up, shook the ring out on to the blotter and regarded it. Well, at least, this assignment hadn't failed. He was suddenly very pleased with himself. By using his brains and these four people as his pawns. he had made half a million dollars within the space of a few days.

He examined the ring closely, then nodded his satisfaction. As he put the ring down, he said, 'I am sure the operation wasn't easy, Mr. Edwards. I am very pleased. In fairness to you, I will double your fee. Let me see . . . it was nine thousand dollars. I will make it eighteen thousand. Is that satisfactory to you?'

Garry shook his head.

'Nine is enough,' he said curtly. 'The less I have of your money, the cleaner I will feel.'

Shalik's eyes snapped, but he shrugged. He opened his desk drawer and took out a long envelope which he tossed across the desk.

Garry picked up the envelope. He didn't bother to check the contents. Putting the envelope in his breast pocket, he got up and walked to the door.

'Mr. Edwards . . .'

Garry paused.

'What is it?'

'I would be glad if you would dictate a full report of what happened during the operation. I would like to have all the details. My secretary will supply you with a tape-recorder.'

'What do you want it for . . . to give to the police?' Garry said. 'You have the ring . . . that's all you're getting from me,' and he went out, walked past the blonde secretary without looking at her and hurried to the elevator, his one thought now being to get back to Toni.

Shalik stared at the closed door, thought for a moment, then shrugged. Perhaps after all, it was better not to know too much about what happened, he decided. Pity about Gaye. He knew she had no relations. There would be no awkward questions asked. She had come into his life, served a useful purpose, and now she had gone. It was a nuisance, but no woman was irreplaceable.

He picked up the ring and examined it. Holding it in his left hand, he reached for his telephone and dialled a number.

The diamonds were nice, he thought and ran his forefinger over the cluster, then started as something of needle sharpness cut his finger. He dropped the ring, frowning, and conveyed his bleeding finger to his mouth.

So the Borgia ring still scratched, he thought. The poison, of course, would have long dried up: after all the ring was nearly four hundred years old. He looked at his finger. Quite a nasty scratch. He continued to suck his finger as he listened to the burr-burr-burr of the telephone bell, thinking how pleased his client would be to get the ring back.